For a ~~long moment, they stared~~ at one another...

Jack looked a little older, but he was still handsome as ever, his wavy dark hair playing around his ears in the breeze. And his eyes, that same light blue that haunted her dreams, bored into her.

She couldn't think what to say. "Hi" seemed silly, with all the unanswered questions and years standing between them.

"I heard you were in town," Jack said, breaking the silence at last.

Amy nodded, not taking her eyes off his. "For a month."

"I was on my way to your house when I saw you two."

She wasn't sure what to say to that. Had it brought up old memories for him, too?

"I'd like to talk, Amy," he said, his voice sounding strained.

Was he hurt, or angry, or both? It was hard to tell exactly how he felt from the way he clenched his jaw, but it was enough to make it clear that he hadn't forgotten about what had happened between them all those years ago.

And now it was time to explain. As much as she wanted to run away again, she wasn't going to.

Dear Reader,

It seems like every new book I write comes with a strange new array of challenges, and this one was no different. Between morning sickness from my current pregnancy and a rambunctious toddler dragging me about by my finger as she explores the world around her, finding the time to write a novel was difficult at times, to say the least.

Still, I was excited to write Amy's story, and as I discovered more about her and Jack, I couldn't wait to discover how they would find their own happily-ever-after. Amy's personality has intrigued me ever since she appeared as Brock's sister in my first Spring Valley story, *The Bull Rider's Twin Trouble*, and I couldn't wait to see what this world wanderer would do while spending a month in her tiny hometown before Brock and Cassie's wedding.

The more books I finish about Spring Valley, the more I want to start, and I hope to give many of the other characters there (especially Brock and Amy's twin brothers) the opportunity to share their stories of finding love. I hope you'll join me as I discover more about each of them, along with all the other people who call Spring Valley home.

Happy reading!

Ali

THE COWBOY'S SURPRISE BABY

ALI OLSON

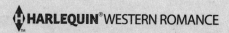

HARLEQUIN®WESTERN ROMANCE

Recycling programs
for this product may
not exist in your area.

ISBN-13: 978-1-335-69965-7

The Cowboy's Surprise Baby

Printed in U.S.A.

Ali Olson is a longtime resident of Las Vegas, Nevada, where she has been teaching English at the high school and college level for the past seven years. Ali has found a passion for writing sexy romance novels, both contemporary and historical, and is enthusiastic about her newly discovered career. She loves reading, writing and traveling with her husband and constant companion, Joe. She appreciates hearing from readers. Write to her at authoraliolson.com.

Books by Ali Olson

Harlequin Western Romance

The Bull Rider's Twin Trouble

Harlequin Blaze

Her Sexy Vegas Cowboy
Her Sexy Texas Cowboy

Visit the Author Profile page
at Harlequin.com for more titles.

To peanut butter and jelly sandwiches.
You got me through the most nauseous moments
of this pregnancy and thus were instrumental
to the completion of this book.

Chapter One

Amy McNeal stepped through the sliding glass doors into the cool autumn air of Texas and breathed it in greedily, ignoring the smell of the exhaust fumes from the waiting cars. After two months in Northern Africa in summer, any temperature below blistering was a refreshing change.

As she walked toward the line of vehicles moving at a snail's pace through the pickup area, her phone started buzzing inside her large travel purse. Amy shifted the suit bag she was carrying to her left hand and dug through the purse with her right, then pulled out her phone and tapped it to answer the call. "Hey! I'm almost at the pickup location," she said.

"I know. I can see you. You better hurry or I'll need to loop around again," answered her brother from the other end.

She looked along the line of cars, trying to peer through the windows for a familiar face. "I don't see you. A little help?"

"I'm in the black truck," he told her.

She rolled her eyes. "This is Texas, Brock. I'm looking at about six black trucks."

"You know, maybe I'll just leave you to find your own way home, if you're going to be like that," he said, but she could hear the smile in his voice and knew she wasn't actually in any danger of being left at the curb.

"Look right. I'm waving out the window," he said.

She spotted him, fifty feet farther along. "I see you! Wait there and I'll be over in a second," she told him.

Amy dropped her phone back into her purse and strode quickly through the crowd of people waiting with their luggage along the curb. When she got to her brother's car, a man in an orange vest was telling him he needed to keep moving, that he wasn't allowed to wait there. "I'm here!" she said breathlessly, slinging her backpack off and into the truck bed, then hopping into the passenger seat.

With a little wave to the airport employee, she settled into her seat and Brock steered them out and away from the airport. "You know we get in trouble here if we sit idling at the curb, right?"

Amy shook her head. "I always forget about how many rules there are in America."

Brock raised an eyebrow and glanced at his sister from the corner of his eye. "If you came home more often, you know, you might remember them."

Amy crossed her arms and turned toward Brock. "You've been back in Spring Valley for two months and already you're starting to sound like Ma," she commented.

"She misses you," he told her, sending a small stab of guilt through her. "It's good to have you back."

Amy gave her brother a smile. "It's good to see you, Brock."

"You're back for the whole month, huh?"

Amy nodded. "I had to be here for my big brother's wedding."

There was a moment of silence, and she knew Brock was waiting for her to say what had happened that made her decide to change her plans and come home so early, rather than just for the weekend of the ceremony. Up until the day before, that had been the plan. But she wasn't ready to explain the events of the last couple weeks, so she stayed silent.

After waiting a few more moments for her to add anything else, Brock said, "Well, I'm glad you'll be around. Be careful, though. You might find yourself deciding to settle down in Spring Valley, regardless of your plans."

Amy snorted. There were at least two very good reasons she would be leaving Spring Valley again. One was her lucrative career as a travel writer, and the other was a handsome cowboy with cornflower-blue eyes. She had some loose ends to tie up with said cowboy, but that didn't mean she'd be sticking around afterward. She was here to set things straight, not make herself miserable. Or him, for that matter.

"Hey, it happens," Brock said defensively.

"Speaking of settling down, how's your fiancée doing?" Amy asked, both because she was interested and because she wanted to change the subject.

Brock looked for a second like he might not accept the topic shift, then gave her a wide grin she didn't remember ever seeing on his face before Cassie came into his life. "She's great, Zach and Carter are great, the ranch is—"

"Great?" Amy said for him.

"Really, really great," he said, nodding, his smile even wider, if that was possible.

"So you don't miss bull riding at all?" she asked, wondering if he'd really given up the rodeo circuit without a qualm.

Brock shook his head decisively. "Not one bit. Giving that up was one of the best decisions I've ever made, and it gives me more time around the people I love. With the wedding, the ranch and twin boys, time is one thing that always seems to be in short supply."

Amy wasn't sure if she believed that Brock didn't miss the rodeo circuit at least a little, but he seemed sincere, so she just had to assume that when he lost his heart, he lost his mind a little, too.

She could remember the rush of riding a horse in the ring, hearing the shouts of the fans, like it was yesterday instead of a decade ago. She had only made it to junior rodeo before dropping out, but that didn't mean it wasn't still a part of her life.

Even after all this time, she still sometimes watched videos of rodeos on her computer when she felt particularly homesick.

But Brock had given it up without a backward glance. Because of love.

Amy had already warned her brother once about the

danger of falling in love, so she didn't say anything now. Still, it worried her. What if it didn't work out for him? She didn't want him to go through that pain. She knew what it felt like to have her whole imagined future with someone come crumbling down around her, and she worried about her brother experiencing the same thing.

Sure, Cassie was wonderful—and they were committing to marriage, after all—but sometimes people who might be perfect for each other still didn't end up together.

"You okay?" Brock asked, breaking into her thoughts.

Amy swallowed the old hurt that was threatening to break the surface and put on a smile. "I'm fine."

For now, at least. After she talked to Jack, though, who knew?

JACK STUART RAN a brush through the chestnut mare's coat, enjoying the feeling of calm it created in him. No matter what else was going on, he could always find some peace around horses. Right this minute, he needed it.

"Any idea how long she'll be around?" he asked his brother.

Tom shrugged his shoulders, not seeming to notice his brother's sudden edginess. "I'm guessing the whole month, up until the wedding. Brock said it was the longest she'd been home since she left for college."

Jack didn't want to tip off his brother about how interested he was, but he couldn't help it. He needed to know everything his brother knew. "Did he say anything else?"

How is she?

Is she seeing anyone?

Does she still think about me after all these years?

"Nope, just that she was coming to town for a bit all of a sudden. The boys tackled him right after, and you know how they are. Had to tell him everything that had happened at their lessons."

Jack didn't say anything, trying to bite off his disappointment that he couldn't learn any more.

"I'm surprised the twins are still coming here at all, to be honest. What with Brock's parents owning a riding school and Brock himself able enough to teach them. Not that I'm complaining of course—we can sure use the business," Tom said, his mind drifting off to other topics besides Amy. "I really think it's only to give those two lovebirds some time alone. Have you seen them together? Don't know if I've ever known two people to be more infatuated with one another."

Oh, Jack did. His older brother had been too busy at college to remember how Jack and Amy had been senior year of high school. Tom knew they'd dated, but not that they'd been in love. Jack and Amy had been planning a life together. Family, careers, everything.

Then, the summer after they graduated, she went off to a university thousands of miles away despite all their plans together, without a word of explanation. He didn't know what had changed or why she decided not to talk to him again. He just knew it still hurt.

And here was his chance to talk to her, hear her side of it, and finally put it all behind him.

As he and Tom left the barn and walked through the twilight toward his childhood home, he felt the itch to get in his truck and drive straight over to see Amy. He would be there in less than five minutes.

The urge almost made him veer toward the side of the house, but he managed to keep himself in check. If she had just gotten home, she was spending time with her family. Not the best time to drive up and demand an explanation.

No, he could wait until tomorrow, Jack told himself.

"Mom loves that you're going to be home for a good long while, you know," Tom said as they neared the house.

Jack could see his mother moving around the kitchen, and he felt a pang of guilt over his desire to drive over to see Amy without a word of explanation to anyone. His mother had likely been cooking up a storm while they were out with the horses.

Jack glanced at his brother, whose mouth was set in a thin line. He knew that Tom was worried about their mother and the ranch she'd lived on for so many years, and that Jack being home wasn't the godsend their mother thought it was, if only because it brought a halt to any extra cash Jack brought in from riding in rodeos.

Tom hadn't been kidding when he'd said they could use any extra business their little riding school could get. As the town had shrunk over the years, so had the number of students they could count on coming to learn to ride. After their father died and Tom moved back to pick up the slack, it had only gotten worse; and Jack knew Tom felt that it was his failings as an instructor that was causing the trouble, despite anything Jack said to the contrary.

Jack hated that he had no idea what he could do about all that. Up until last week he'd tried to help by sending home what he could from his earnings on the circuit, but even that never seemed to be enough. He was sure he could become a real champion if the cards fell right, and then they could stop worrying so much, but for that he needed a great partner and a whole lot of luck—two things that hadn't seemed to come his way lately.

His old partner was decent, but since he broke his leg and decided to call it quits, Jack wasn't sure what he'd do. No partner, no rodeos. No rodeos, no money.

He loved being home on the ranch he hoped to run one day, but now he needed to find someone to rope with. It was the type of decision that could make or break his career. All that on his plate, and now there was Tom to help, too. It was a tall order.

And now he had Amy McNeal to think about. His stay in Spring Valley was already getting much more complicated than he'd expected just a few days ago.

As THE SUN dipped behind the mountains ringing Spring Valley, Amy lowered herself carefully from Brock's truck until her feet were planted securely on the gravel driveway of their parents' old sprawling ranch house. The last time she'd come home, she'd fallen and twisted her ankle badly doing that very thing, and she wasn't about to go through that again. If Cassie, who was a doctor and lived next door, hadn't taken care of her, she might have ended up missing her departure flight last time.

Amy turned her attention from her feet to the group of people standing on the front porch. Cassie was already there, with her twin sons, and Ma and Pop, all happy to see her. Amy felt a twinge of homesickness, which was silly. She *was* home, after all.

Cassie, Brock's fiancée, came down and gave Amy a tight hug. Even though they had only met up a couple times during Amy's last stay, and that was when she was still just the neighbor, Cassie had been kind and friendly from the start.

"How's your ankle?" she asked the moment she and Amy broke apart.

"Good, most of the time. Just gives me the odd twinge if I step down wrong," Amy said, glad to have a doctor in the family.

Cassie nodded sympathetically, but it was clear there wasn't much to be done about it. Just another sign that she wasn't in her teens anymore.

The cool evening breeze ruffled Amy's hair, and she wished she had a jacket. Living out of a backpack for years, she'd learned to just buy occasional items as she needed them, and she certainly hadn't needed anything heavier than a light sweater in nearly a year, following the summer and staying on tropical islands or in deserts.

She might need to buy a coat. But for the time being,

she would just borrow something from her mother, however grandmotherly her Ma's wardrobe was—and it had been since she'd adopted Amy, if the pictures were any indication.

Ma herself rushed forward and pulled Amy into a tight hug, and Amy felt her heart swell with the feeling of home. As much as she avoided Spring Valley, she missed it, and the people. "Hi, Ma," she said, hoping the older woman wasn't going to cry.

Ma was a tough lady, but she never could understand why Amy was gone so much, and it hurt Amy to see the toll it took on her. To avoid it, Amy rummaged in her bag and pulled out two packages, handing one to Ma and the other to Cassie. "They're some different spices and a grinder," she explained.

Cassie thanked her, but Ma looked skeptical. "Smell them and give them a shot," Amy said, sure her adopted mother would manage to make something magical and somehow still completely Southern with them.

Then Amy turned to her soon-to-be nephews. "I brought y'all spices, too!" she told them.

"You did?" Carter asked, not sounding too enthused at the idea.

"No. I want to be your favorite aunt, and I have some catching up to do, so I brought you fez hats and drums," she said, pulling out the items and handing them to the boys.

Zach immediately began giggling to see the funny little hat on his brother, and they both started hitting the drums enthusiastically. Brock appeared at Amy's elbow. "Drums? Really?" he asked his little sister.

Amy shrugged. "There were some really cool knives I considered getting them. This seemed like the better choice."

Brock and Cassie winced at the noise. "I'm not so sure about that," Brock commented.

Cassie whispered quickly to Zach and Carter, and they both ran over to Amy, giving her a big hug. "Thanks, Aunt Amy," they said in unison.

Amy nodded to them, fighting tears. She didn't want to admit how much it twisted her heart to be around these two sweet boys. They reminded her too much of truths she didn't like to think about.

"Time to get inside," Ma said, ushering everyone through the door. "Dinner's ready and will start getting cold any minute."

Amy, thankful for the interruption, followed the rest of them inside after giving Pop a quick hug. She only paused at the door for a second, looking in the direction of Stuart Ranch, and wondering what her life would be like if things had been just a little different.

Suddenly, she wished she was on a plane to Panama. Or Indonesia. Heck, Idaho would work. Anywhere, so long as it was a couple thousand miles from the painful memories that were threatening to come back to the surface now that she was here.

But those painful memories were the reason she was here, so she bit back the desire to flee and walked inside her childhood home, closing the door behind her.

Amy soon found herself sitting down at her parents' table, already piled high with Ma's famous cooking. "So, update me on what's going on with everyone," she said, hoping talk would keep her mind from wandering back toward Stuart Ranch.

"Pop's working himself too hard fixing the barn when he could just let me do it. Or hire someone," Brock began as they all began filling their plates.

Pop cut into Brock's scolding. "I'm not so old I can't lift a hammer, Brock," he said around his mustache. "And the horses will appreciate it, which is good for the riding school."

Pop had always been such a strong, consistent force in her life that it was hard for Amy to imagine him ever slowing down, but she could see that Brock was concerned. Still, he didn't seem willing to push the topic any further than he already had.

"Speaking of riding," Brock said, pointing to the twins, "these two have been doing a great job learning to ride and care for horses."

Zach and Carter beamed. "Mr. Stuart says we're naturals," Carter declared.

Amy about choked on her water. "Stuart?" she asked in between coughs.

Brock nodded, looking proud. "Tom Stuart's taken over the school since his father passed a year ago. The boys go there twice a week."

Amy's heart started again. She hadn't known the boys were going to the Stuarts', and hearing the name out of the blue like that had done more to her than she liked to admit. She suddenly hoped to heaven that Jack was still out on the circuit. Maybe he would even be gone the entire month she was there, and she could board her plane to Thailand after the wedding and just forget about her resolution to speak to him, which seemed awfully daunting now that she was home.

Brock gestured to her with his fork. "Jack's back in town right now, too. Weren't you two an item for a while in high school?"

Amy felt her heart jolt again at the sound of his name. Of course, Brock had been on the rodeo circuit when they'd started dating. He didn't know how serious their relationship had been, didn't know that his name cut through her like a knife.

But Ma and Pop knew some of it. Pop stood, clearing his throat, and all the attention turned to him. "I just want to thank y'all for being here. It does an old man good to see so many people he loves around the table together."

There was a round of "hear, hear!" and a lifting of glasses, and then Pop sat back down. "Now, stop with the chatter and get to eatin'. I don't plan on having leftovers," Ma added.

With that, they tucked in, eating heartily. Amy didn't look at Brock, in case he decided to start up the conversation again. She did, however, risk a glance at Pop, who was looking at her with concern. Amy gave him a little nod of thanks, then turned her eyes back to the plate in front of her.

Jack Stuart was in town right this minute, just a few miles away. When she'd bought her ticket to come home, she had hoped he would be, but now...

The mix of emotions he evoked was too much to analyze. All she knew for sure was that she couldn't run and hide any longer, and she needed to be prepared to talk to him. Tell him the truth.

AMY AWOKE LONG before sunrise, her internal clock still not quite on Texas time. Once awake, her mind immediately turned to Jack, her stomach twisting. She lay in bed wondering if he already knew she was home, if he would decide to confront her about her disappearance after graduation, or if she would be the one to seek him out. And if she could force herself to actually do so.

She knew that her eighteen-year-old self hadn't handled things particularly well, and she still felt guilt rise in her when she thought of the messages he had left, asking her to please call him and tell him why she hadn't talked to him, why she had just left without saying goodbye.

She had listened to each one over and over again, torturing herself just so she could hear his voice, but she hadn't had the nerve to call him back, to talk to him, to explain why she'd gone away.

She was stronger now, though. She had made the decision to come clean to him, and she *could* handle it, however difficult it might seem. After all, their relationship had been a long time ago. About a decade now. Shouldn't that be long enough to wipe away everything that had happened between them?

She knew, though, that it hadn't been long enough for her.

Amy sighed and pulled herself out of bed, determined to get her mind off her high school sweetheart.

For an hour, she struggled to write an article about her experiences in the Sahara Desert, but the camels and tribesmen and women felt impossible to capture in words when her brain was so full of other things so much closer to home.

Finally, frustrated, she turned from her laptop and paced the length of her small childhood bedroom, trying to get her mind to settle down and focus. She felt too closed in to think properly—that was the problem, she told herself.

Amy could see that the sky had lightened enough for the world outside her window to be more than just a swath of darkness, and she determined that it would be best to get out of this tiny room. Her eyes landed on her old tan Stetson, hanging on one of her bedposts, just where she would always put it after a ride, and she smiled.

In a couple of minutes, her hair was falling down her back underneath a battered cowboy hat, and she had thrown on her jeans. With her old cowboy boots in one hand, she sneaked quietly down the stairs in just her socks, hoping not to wake anyone.

Once she was standing outside and the back door was shut behind her, she slid her feet into her boots and walked quickly toward the barn, feeling like a younger version of herself. When she reached it, it took no time at all to slip inside and find her old tack in its place against the wall. Pa had taken good care of it while she was gone.

The smell of hay and the nickering of horses surrounded her and was a soothing presence, and for a moment she stood there, feeling the supple leather of her saddle and remembering old times when she wanted nothing more than to live on a ranch and ride in rodeos. And marry Jack.

She turned from the saddle, wishing she could turn from her thoughts as easily, and walked along the row of horses. Since the family ran a riding school, there was no shortage of animals to ride, but she still looked over them all, telling herself she wasn't looking for Bandit.

Bandit had been her horse back in the day, a beautiful black stallion with white freckled markings on his nose, and when he died during her first year of college, she'd cried long and hard. It still sent a pang through her heart to think of him, and she knew she would always wonder if he'd felt abandoned when she moved so far away.

Bandit wasn't there, of course, and she looked over the horses once again, this time seeing them as they were, and not what they weren't. A feisty-looking mare, dark brown, butted Amy with her nose, stopping her in her tracks. When Amy looked the animal in the eyes, she knew they'd get along just fine.

Amy saddled up the mare, whose name she didn't know, and walked her out of the barn. In the early-morning light, the mare's coat shone a deep bronze, and Amy patted her. "What do you say we go for a ride, girl?" she asked.

The horse snorted and pulled her head up quickly, almost as if she was nodding. Amy grinned at her and mounted the animal, settling into the saddle as if she'd only been riding the day before. With that, the two were off around the property, getting to know each other.

For a few minutes, Amy was content to ride at a walking pace as she accustomed herself to the mare's gait. Once she was comfortable, though, she started to feel antsy. The lingering anxiety was still there, nagging at the back of her mind, and she decided to do what she'd always done to clear her mind in the old days: outrun her thoughts. Amy turned the mare toward the fence line, and in a few seconds they were through a small gate and onto a trail that wound its way through the trees that bordered her parents' property.

Soon Amy and the mare were moving at a quick trot along the footpath. Amy leaned close to the mare's neck as she reveled in the familiar feeling. She must have traveled along this trail hundreds of times when she was in high school, exercising the horses and leading children from her father's riding school along the path.

When they broke through the last of the trees into an open field, Amy urged the horse to go faster, and they streaked through the short grass at a run, hurtling along until they reached a dirt road. The feel of her hair streaming behind her as the cool wind slapped her face gave Amy more joy than she remembered feeling in a long time. When they slowed, she took in a deep breath and shivered with the cold.

By that time the sky was full of light, and Amy

knew it was probably time to get back. She turned the mare to walk along the road, back toward the ranch.

Amy was still breathing hard, her heart pounding, when she saw something that made it beat even harder. A few hundred yards up the road was a truck, a cowboy leaning against it and watching her.

She knew the truck and the cowboy so well, she recognized them immediately, even though it had been a decade since she'd seen either one. How many times had she looked up from a ride to see that cowboy leaning just that way on that beat-up old truck?

Without any guidance, the horse continued walking toward the ranch, bringing Amy closer and closer to Jack Stuart. She couldn't bring herself to look away from him, and he kept his eyes locked on hers.

This was it. She'd promised herself she would do this, and now the time had come. Amy took a long, calming breath.

After what felt like an eternity, the mare was only a few feet from the truck. Amy pulled on the reins and the horse stopped and waited to be told what to do next. Amy wished someone would tell her what she should do, too, but she knew she'd need to figure it out for herself.

Jack moved away from the truck and came closer, stroking the horse's muzzle, still keeping his eyes on Amy. For a long moment, they stared at one another, only a foot of space between them.

If her heart hadn't been beating so hard, it might have stopped at the sight of Jack so close. He looked a little older, but he was still handsome as ever, his wavy dark hair playing around his ears in the breeze. And his eyes, that same light blue that haunted her dreams, bored into her.

She couldn't think of what to say. *Hi* seemed silly, with all the unanswered questions and years standing between them.

"I heard you were in town," Jack said, breaking the silence at last.

Amy nodded, not taking her eyes off his. "For a month."

"I was on my way to your house when I saw you two."

She wasn't sure what to say to that. Had it brought up old memories for him, too?

"I'd like to talk, Amy," he said, his voice sounding strained.

Was he hurt, or angry, or both? It was hard to tell exactly how he felt from the way he clenched his jaw, but it was enough to make it clear that he hadn't forgotten about what had happened between them all those years ago.

And now it was time to explain. As much as she wanted to run away again, she wasn't going to. The mare snorted and shifted beneath her, as if she could feel Amy's roil of emotions.

Her eyes began to sting with the tears of all the years she'd missed with him because of the hand fate had dealt her.

Chapter Two

Jack hated what seeing her did to his heart. She had dumped him—even worse, just avoided him—yet when he looked at her all he wanted to do was pull her into his arms. The moment he'd seen her as he was driving along, her blond hair flying along behind her just like it did when she rode junior rodeo in high school, it was like the last decade had never happened.

It was even worse when she looked down at him from her perch on the horse, her green eyes sparkling with tears. He couldn't meet them and keep his distance. He turned his eyes to the truck. "How about we sit for a few minutes?" he asked, lowering the tailgate of his truck.

It would be warmer in the cab, but he knew Amy would want to keep close to the horse. Besides, he didn't think he could be in that small a space with her and keep his wits about him. As it was, he already felt claustrophobic despite the wide-open sky and the large animal between them.

Amy swung herself off the horse, wincing when she dropped her weight onto one foot, and if he'd been any closer, he would have automatically put his arms on her waist to steady her. He was almost glad for the distance between them, since he wasn't sure what touching her would do to him. "Are you okay?" he asked.

She nodded. "Twisted my ankle a while back, and it still gives me trouble sometimes."

Jack almost said something, anything, to keep the conversation away from the tough stuff, but he kept his mouth shut. It was finally time to talk about what had happened between them.

Amy seemed to think the same thing, because she walked over and sat down on the tailgate, reins in her hand, and sighed. "For what it's worth, I'm sorry. About not calling you," she said, her voice quieter, softer than he remembered ever hearing it before. "I was a coward not to talk to you about what was going on."

He waited while she took a deep breath, and for a brief moment he considered stopping her right there. If whatever she was going to say took a decade to come out, maybe he didn't want to hear it. Maybe, if she never said anything, they could just start where they'd left off...

He brushed away the crazy idea. He needed to know.

"A few days after graduation, while you were gone on your family trip, I went to the doctor."

His mind filled with possibilities, some of them terrifying, though none of them made sense. Was she sick? If she had been ill for the last decade, she certainly didn't show it. She looked as beautiful as she had at seventeen, even more so, with the air of confidence she seemed to exude now, even when she was near tears.

Had she gotten pregnant? That seemed like an odd reason for her to run from him, since she would have known, even at that young age, that he would be more than happy to raise a child with her. They had been talking about having a family together nearly the entire time they were together.

His mind flitted back to illness. What if she *was* sick? Deathly sick? And he didn't know?

He waited, the pit of his stomach tense, for what the doctor might have told her that had made her disappear from his life.

"I found out that I can't have kids, Jack. Ever. I left because you deserved to be with someone who could give you the family you've always wanted."

Jack felt a combination of pain and relief. He turned to look carefully at Amy. "But you're not sick or anything?" he asked.

"Except for not being able to have children, I'm fine—"

"It's *you* I cared about, Amy, not whether or not you can make babies. Hell, you're adopted. You know better than anyone that there are other options, if we wanted kids."

Jack had never felt so relieved, yet at the same time he was sad for all the years together they had lost. Sure, he'd wanted kids, but this was Amy. What he'd always wanted, more than anything, was *her*.

Amy still looked somber. "You say that now, Jack,

and I know you would've said that then, but the years would have gone by and you'd have wished we could have children. *Your* children. Even if you didn't, I'd always wonder if you did. I didn't want that to fester underneath the surface, ruining our relationship."

"So you left?" Jack asked, searching her face.

Amy looked away from his eyes. She seemed embarrassed. "I couldn't break up with you. I know I never would've been able to make myself say the words to you. And since I couldn't let myself stay with you, leaving felt like my only option. I'm sorry for doing that to you, Jack. I was a coward. You deserved better."

At last, a great weight disappeared from Jack's shoulders. After years of wondering, at least he knew the answers to all his unanswered questions. Now there still seemed to be one question left: Where did he go from there?

AMY SAT ON the tailgate, chilled by the early-morning breeze and by her own thoughts. She waited for him to say something that would give her a clue as to what he was thinking. If he despised her cowardice, wanted nothing to do with her, she deserved it. She wouldn't run from it anymore. She patted the mare's soft muzzle absentmindedly, waiting.

Finally, he spoke. "We should get your horse back to the barn," he said, hopping off the tailgate and holding out his hand to her. "How about we walk there? I can come back for the truck."

She was speechless for a moment. The unexpected friendliness, the opening of a door she thought long closed, surprised her. When she took his hand, however, its warmth and steadiness rushed through her, and the spark of recognition and comfort that flowed through the link made her smile. Her hand felt right nestled in his, like they had never been apart.

"Your hands are freezing," Jack commented, pressing hers in both of his.

She was warmed by more than his palms as he helped her stand, and their fingers lingered together for an extra moment before he let go to close his tailgate and pull his keys from the ignition.

They began walking side by side toward her parents' ranch along the road, the mare walking along behind them and occasionally batting Amy with her nose, as if anxious to move faster. Amy, though, wasn't in any rush to finish the half mile or so walk. She didn't want this intimate moment to be over too quickly.

"I can't believe you still have that old truck," she told Jack, glancing back at the vehicle parked beside the field. "After all the times it broke down in high school, I never would have imagined it would last so long."

"I had to put a lot of work into it over the years, and it still has a few quirks," Jack said, giving her a sidelong smile that went straight to her heart, "but I've loved it since I was a teenager. I could never just give up on it."

Amy blushed, feeling the words resonate through her, sure he was talking about more than just the truck.

But no. Even if they did, the facts of the situation had not changed. She still couldn't have children, and he still deserved the chance to find a woman who could give him the family he'd always wanted.

He had the chance, and it seems he never took it, she thought to herself. She couldn't stop the heat from blossoming in her chest. It turned to ice as she put back up the walls she'd built around her heart in the past few days. She knew now better than ever that she couldn't let herself get carried away with a man. Even if it was Jack.

He stopped walking and turned toward her, and she did the same. Suddenly, she felt as if he was much too close, and at the same time too far away, and she longed to move closer. To touch his lips with hers. She took a step back.

She was sure the feel of their lips, their bodies, together would also be on the list of things that hadn't changed, and it scared her.

"Will you go out with me tonight?" he asked, his voice low and deep.

The word *yes* was on her tongue, but Amy balked. She couldn't let them fall right back into the relationship she'd run away from, could she? What about all that had happened since? Would there just be too much between them? And she had no idea who he was now. He could be every bit as despicable as Armand, the person she least wanted to think about.

Jack seemed to realize her indecision, because he turned and started walking toward her house again. After a moment, she pulled herself out of her shock and hustled to catch up with him. When he spoke, he sounded lighthearted, confident. Exactly the Jack she knew from high school. "How about this—we go out tonight just to get to know each other. We start fresh. No expectations. No baggage. No past. Just us, two twentysomethings who met while I was out for a drive and you were going for a ride on your horse."

She had to smile at his antics. "No past? So you saw a random woman riding a horse in the middle of nowhere and stopped to ask her out?"

His eyes danced with laughter. "When you put it like that, it doesn't sound so great. How about I was driving along when I saw a beautiful woman and a beautiful horse, and I felt compelled to speak to her. The woman, not the horse."

Amy wasn't sure if she was amused or panicked. For a moment he sounded just like Armand. Charming, flattering…but this was *Jack*. He was being sincere.

Wasn't he?

They grew quiet and walked a little longer, until her childhood home appeared down the street.

"So I'll pick you up tonight at seven?" he said, his voice serious as he turned toward her again.

Amy nodded, though a large part of her yelled that it was too much, too soon. Jack's face lit with a smile, and he turned his attention back to the house that loomed before them. She was glad he wasn't looking at her any longer, so he wouldn't see just how torn and confused she was.

She tried to tell herself she was being stupid, worrying over nothing. She'd known Jack almost as long as she'd been alive. Armand was—well, he was a blip on the radar of her life, not worth thinking about. So she would just stop.

The likelihood of that was so far-fetched that Amy couldn't stop a snort from escaping.

"What're you thinking about over there?" Jack asked, the gleam in his eye making him so devilishly handsome she wasn't sure if she wanted to kiss him or run away.

"That wasn't me, that was the horse," she said, turning away so he wouldn't see the flow of emotions she couldn't control.

He snorted skeptically in response, and she felt the tension inside her break as a laugh broke from her throat. She'd forgotten how easily he could make her laugh, regardless of her mood. She had missed that.

They arrived at the house, and even though the mare was pulling Amy toward the barn, she couldn't pull herself away from Jack, as if something magnetic about him forced her to stay close to him now that she'd found him again.

He looked in her eyes again, making her stomach drop somewhere near her toes. "Seven, right?" he asked.

The note of insecurity in his voice sent a pang through her heart. It reminded her again of how much she must have hurt him. She nodded. "Seven."

He leaned forward and brushed his lips against hers, sending a shock wave of hormones rushing through her body. Her mind recoiled at the feeling, and she almost called the date off right then and there. The idea of being vulnerable again so soon, even with Jack, made her more than nervous.

Jack seemed to realize he'd crossed the line. He tilted his hat and said, "I don't normally kiss ladies I just met. I assure you, I'll be a perfect gentleman on our date."

He turned back toward the road and began walking away, but she wasn't ready for him to disappear. Not quite yet.

"You haven't even asked my name," she called to him, desperate to see his face again for a few more seconds.

He looked at her with a smile and bowed. "Where are my manners? Name's Jack, miss. And you are…?" he asked.

God, he was so cute she could hardly speak. "Amelia. Friends call me Amy."

"Amelia," he repeated, as if tasting the word, and she felt such an overwhelming urge to kiss him she was glad he was already several feet away.

Reluctantly, she started toward the barn, following the horse's insistent pull. Before she could get too far, though, she realized something. "This is all I have to wear for a date," she said to his retreating figure, raising her voice so he would hear and gesturing toward her jeans and old T-shirt. "I've been living out of a backpack in the African desert for the past year."

He just smiled at her again. "Sounds like you'll have some mighty interesting stories to tell me at dinner, miss. You can just wear that," he said, eyeing her carefully. "I like the cowgirl look."

Before she could say anything in response, Jack had chuckled and waved. "See you at seven," he called as he turned away a final time.

Once he was gone, she spun toward the barn and practically ran the rest of the way, making the horse move quickly to keep up. Even so, Amy was unable to outrun her thoughts.

What was the matter with her? Jack was *not* Armand. He wasn't the type of guy to seduce her and manipulate her into falling for him. He wasn't a selfish liar. He was Jack.

Still, she couldn't seem to stop herself from panicking every time he said something sweet or she felt desire rise up.

She knew she was still hurting from what she'd been through, and that it was far too soon to go on a date with Jack. She knew she should've said no. But it was too late now, and a part of her wanted so badly to be with him again, to feel his arms around her. To be safe and secure.

She was going on a date. That was all there was to it. They would talk and eat and get to know each other again. And maybe, maybe she would be able to convince herself that everything that had happened in Morocco was in the past.

As she brushed down the mare, Amy went over the morning's events once more in her head. Jack was just as attractive as always, that was for sure, but in high school he'd seemed a little more…happy-go-lucky, she supposed. He had always seemed happy, as if life smiled upon him. There was something care-worn about him now.

She fervently hoped that she wasn't the one to change that about him.

She shook her head at the irony of that thought, since it was just that part of his nature that had been one of the reasons she had run instead of talking to him. She'd been worried he would convince her that the doctors were wrong and they could have exactly the life they'd planned because it was the life he *wanted*, dammit, and everything always worked out the way he wanted.

And she had known all those years ago that if she talked to him she would cave, give in to the hope even when she knew the odds, and it had made her a coward.

But now—

"I saw Jack Stuart walking you home," Pop said from behind Amy, startling her out of her thoughts.

He came up beside her and pet the horse she was grooming, but said nothing else. Just waited.

Amy nodded. "He spotted me while I was out riding. We had a good talk."

Pop said nothing, but she could tell by the slight curve of his mustache that he was pleased. He didn't meddle in the affairs of his children like Ma, but he cared deeply for their happiness. Impulsively, Amy gave the old man a hug.

"I don't know if it's a good idea or not, but I'm going on a date with him tonight. I've missed him all these years, but maybe this is a bad idea. Maybe I'm just setting myself up to get hurt, and I don't want to go through that again—" She stopped, aware she was saying more than she'd meant to.

She hadn't told anyone about Armand, and frankly she didn't plan on doing it anytime soon. It was more than humiliating, and she wasn't ready to relive it.

Luckily, Pop wasn't the type to pry. He put a hand on Amy's shoulder. "Don't you worry," he said.

She wasn't sure if he meant not to worry about the date or her past pain or what, but it was fine not knowing. He probably meant all of it. Pop didn't need many words to be there for his daughter.

Amy turned back to the mare to finish grooming her. "How's the riding school going?" she asked, ready for a change of topic.

The old man puffed out a stream of air that made his mustache flutter. "Fewer kids every year, seems like. If it weren't for the rest of the ranch and the few stud horses we have, it wouldn't be worth the costs. Still, it's such a part of this place I'd keep it going if it cost me a small fortune. Your ma thinks I'm crazy, but there it is."

Amy hadn't heard her father say so many words in one go since the time he'd lectured her on the dangers of peer pressure when she was a teenager. She'd always known her pop was partial to the riding school, and even though she worried about his health, she had to love his loyalty to the horses and the children.

The mare under Amy's hand snorted and shook her mane, as if trying to get Amy's attention back on her where it belonged. Amy smiled. "I like this horse, Pop. What's her name?"

"Queen Bee."

Amy chuckled as the animal raised her head regally. The name fit her, certainly.

"Be careful riding her, though. She had a run-in with a snake a while back and spooks easy. I don't let the riding school kids take her out anymore."

Amy patted the horse like she was an old friend. "I can handle a skittish horse, Pop."

JACK DROVE BACK to his family's ranch in a state of disbelief. He had prepared himself for an ugly fight, or for no answer at all, but not this. A reconciliation? Maybe not quite, but it was at least a new chance for him and Amy.

He also hadn't been prepared for all the emotions he would feel when he saw her. He'd tried to be ready, but nothing he could have done would prepare him for the electricity that shot through him at the sight of her. She was as stunning as ever.

There was also a sliver of fear, as if she was going to disappear again before his eyes, as if she had never been real in the first place.

He drummed his fingers on the steering wheel, full of nervous energy. He didn't know what he could do to keep himself occupied until that evening, but he'd need to find something or he would go crazy waiting, wondering if it was all real, if she would be there when he arrived at the McNeal house at seven.

Once his truck was parked in front of Stuart Ranch, Jack went immediately toward the barn, veering around the house. Indoors sounded stifling, and he knew it would be infuriating to pace around the living room watching the hand on the clock move with frustrating slowness, which he was sure would happen. Better to get onto a horse and do something under the clear cool sky rather than hole up inside.

As he approached the barn, his brother Tom walked out with a couple of horses on leads. Jack went up to him, seeing an opportunity for distraction. "How can I help?" he asked.

Tom gave him a curious look, as if he sensed something of Jack's emotions. "I'm setting up for a group of students. They'll be here in a half hour."

"Ages?" Jack asked, turning to go to the barn and get whatever else they might need for the riding lessons.

"Under sevens," Tom answered. "There'll be about four kids total," he added before Jack could disappear into the barn.

Jack sighed. He should have expected such low numbers, but it was always a little deflating to be reminded how much it had dwindled. With more than one school in this tiny area, and the drop in population over the past few years, having any students at all was a stroke of luck. His father and Mr. McNeal had started their riding schools years ago when the high demand for lessons meant both schools could prosper. When their father was, if not young, at least spry, they had kids driving in from towns over an hour away. He loved teaching children how to ride, and it showed in the flourishing school he ran.

Without his touch, the school had fallen off to

maybe twenty students. If Spring Valley's population had stayed steady, maybe they would be afloat even without Dad's magic touch, but as the town dwindled, so did their business.

Now they were at the point that the only reason they'd manage to pay the bills was Jack's winnings from the rodeo and Tom's determination to stretch every dollar. If Jack didn't find a new partner soon, he didn't think even Tom's penny-pinching would save them.

Still, the ranch had to run. It was their mom's home—it was Jack's future. Tom didn't want the ranch, never had, but Jack always dreamed of turning it into a rodeo school when he retired with a good chunk of cash from his roping career.

If they could somehow last that long. Something would need to change, but what and how?

Jack pulled himself out of his reverie. It wasn't helping anything, and he'd gone over it all so many times, but it always led to nothing. Now was the time to work, not think, so he grabbed a couple more of their gentlest horses and brought them out to the paddock where Tom was standing with the others.

They looped the leads over a fence post and both went back for saddles. "Have a good drive?" Tom asked.

Jack could tell Tom wanted to ask what had happened, knew Tom saw a change in him. And even though there was no reason to hide his reunion with Amy, that their date couldn't possibly be a secret, he still felt a momentary desire to hide it, as if talking about it might make it all go away like a birthday wish or something.

Tom was watching him, though, and he knew he had to come clean. "I went to see Amy. We talked and decided to go out tonight."

"Like on a date?" Tom asked, sounding a little surprised.

"I guess so," Jack answered, not ready to clarify more.

He loved his brother, but talking had never been their strong suit, and it seemed strange to open up to him about the real history of his relationship with Amy and what this date could or could not mean. Heck, he wasn't even really ready to *think* about all that, let alone *talk* about it.

Tom seemed to understand, because he didn't ask anything more, and soon they were guiding little kids around the paddock, each one practicing squeezing their legs to make their horse go and pulling on the reins to stop. The two youngest children, identical twins, could hardly manage enough force to get the horse's attention, but the docile creatures listened to them with the patience of loving parents.

Jack watched the twins with interest. Zach and Carter, Brock's soon-to-be sons, had settled into Spring Valley comfortably and seemed more than ready to add Brock to their family. He'd seen the way their faces lit up around Amy's brother. They loved him and from what Jack had seen, Brock clearly doted on them. Jack had always wanted a family, and it made his heart swell to think that a child didn't need to be yours biologically in order to be family.

Like the McNeal clan. All four children were adopted, and their parents loved every one of them as much as any parent could. If a couple were unable to have children for some reason…

His mind balked as Jack realized he had drifted into territory he wasn't remotely ready for. He had only seen Amy for a few minutes after ten years of complete silence from her—there was no way he should be thinking about them starting a family together. Heck, part of him was still dead sure dinner was a bad idea. The part that had never healed when she left the first time.

He wasn't ready to get hurt like that again, and thoughts like those would only make it worse.

Still, he couldn't help but watch the time tick by oh so slowly toward seven, and he did everything he could think of to speed it along.

He hadn't been this antsy for a date in a very long time. About ten years, in fact.

Chapter Three

Amy sat with Cassie, the two women shading their eyes against the afternoon light as they watched Brock play tag with the young twins, while the new cows lowed happily in the pen Brock had built over the past two months. If Amy hadn't been so preoccupied with thoughts of her date in just a few hours, the antics of the three males would have been hilarious. As it was, though, she was hardly able to even hold a basic conversation with Cassie, let alone anything else.

After the third time Amy had to apologize for not hearing what Cassie had said, Cassie gave her an intense clinical stare. "Is everything okay, Amy? You're almost as difficult to talk to as Brock was when he had a concussion. Did you hit your head recently? Who was the first President of the United States?"

Amy chuckled and shook her head. "I don't have a concussion, Cassie. I'm just...preoccupied."

"With what?" Cassie asked, her demeanor shifting from doctor to sister instantaneously.

Amy didn't have any sisters—well, didn't grow up with any, at least, she amended—so it felt odd to con-

fide in Cassie like this, but she needed to talk to someone. Pop was a good listener but not one for advice and
long conversations, and Ma would end up trying to
play the ultimate matchmaker if she even got a whiff
of an opportunity. Amy took a breath and spilled her
thoughts to her soon-to-be sister-in-law.

"Do you know Jack Stuart?" she asked, knowing
the answer.

"Sure," Cassie said. "He was at the riding school
with Tom today for the boys' lesson. Zach said he is,
and I quote, 'a really cool rodeo cowboy.'"

Amy agreed with Zach's assessment, but it didn't
even scratch the surface of everything there was to
say about Jack.

"He's also my high school sweetheart, my first boyfriend," Amy added. "He's taking me out tonight and
I'm just a bit nervous. It's been a long time since we've
seen each other and so much has changed and Jack—"
Amy cut off the torrent of words, not sure what she
wanted to say.

Jack was special.

Jack could be a chance to start over.

Jack didn't know who she was and what she'd done,
and she wasn't sure he'd still like her when he found
out.

Cassie seemed to have filled in the blank her own
way, because she hopped up and grabbed Amy's hand,
pulling her inside. "If you've got a date, we have much
more important things to do than sit here watching
three guys tumbling around the yard. Do you even have
any nice clothes in that backpack of yours?"

Amy smiled as Cassie's enthusiasm calmed some of her worries. "Nothing but travel clothes, jeans and a few summer dresses. Jack won't care what I'm wearing but—"

"But you do, of course," Cassie said before Amy could finish the sentence. "I'm a bit shorter than you, but I bet a few of my things will fit. Want to go shopping in my closet?"

Amy nodded, relieved she would have something to wear that hadn't been tainted by her recent past. Amy cut that thought off before it could gain any more traction and followed Cassie. In a few minutes they were ankle-deep in discarded dresses. Each one had been pronounced too something for this date. Too conservative. Too risqué. Too formal. Too short.

Finally, Cassie clapped her hands in delight, and Amy had to agree. She was holding a knee-length dress in a shimmery navy blue with little cap sleeves that Amy loved. "Go try it on," Cassie urged, and Amy took the dress into the bathroom.

When she stepped back out, Cassie's squeal of happiness confirmed her thoughts: it was a beautiful dress.

"He's going to fall in love with you the moment he sees you," Cassie said dreamily.

The thought made her heart stutter. Did she want him to fall in love with her again? The thought sent a wave of fear through her, and she knew she wasn't ready to talk about anything resembling love.

"What's wrong, Amy? This isn't about the dress, is it?" Cassie asked, putting her hand on Amy's arm.

Amy sat on the bed, feeling sudden tears spring

into her eyes. Cassie sat beside her. "You can tell me anything, Amy. Doctor-patient confidentiality," she added with a smile.

"Are you a therapist?" Amy asked with a little laugh as she brushed a tear away.

"Not technically, but I can sure try, if that's what you need."

Amy sighed. "In Morocco, I met a man. Armand. He was—"

She searched for the right word while Cassie waited patiently. "He was incredibly charming," Amy finally finished, though that didn't really do justice to the pull he had over her.

"I gather it didn't end well?" Cassie prompted quietly.

Amy laughed. "That's the understatement of the century. He wasn't who I thought he was. He was married, for one thing."

Cassie pulled Amy into a hug, and Amy was grateful she didn't have to explain any more about her relationship with Armand. The way he manipulated her feelings, the way he'd treated her after he'd known she was hooked. How difficult it had been to get back her independence and leave.

"Anyway, I got away from all that and came home. And now I'm going on this date and feel like a complete basket case for even agreeing to it after all that," Amy said, trying to end the conversation and stop herself from becoming completely overwhelmed with still-fresh feelings at the same time.

Cassie gave her a look of concern. "You can still call

off or postpone this date if it's too much for you, you know. This dress will wait, and I'm sure Jack would understand."

Amy only thought about that for a second before dismissing it. There was no way she was going to cancel this date. "I need this date, I think. It might help me get rid of Armand, but mostly…" She paused, struggling for words. "It's *Jack*," she finished, sure Cassie couldn't understand everything he meant to her. Heck, she didn't think she did, either.

"Well, if you're going on a date tonight, we need to figure out something for shoes, because I don't think mine will fit you," Cassie declared, shaking her head.

Amy smiled, glad the conversation had turned to less serious topics. She looked at her feet and knew instinctively what shoes she wanted to wear with this dress. "Shoes I've got taken care of. Thanks so much for the help, Cassie. And for listening. I promise next time we'll talk about fun things like your wedding instead of having a therapy session."

Cassie shrugged and started picking up the discarded dresses. "It's no problem. I mean, how can I ask you to be my bridesmaid if I'm not willing to be a shoulder to cry on once in a while? I'll probably need you to return the favor as the big day approaches and the inevitable wedding disasters occur."

Amy's eyes widened in surprise. "You want me to be one of your bridesmaids?"

Cassie looked up. "Of course I want you to be a bridesmaid. I was hoping to have three. Emma from the bakery, my sister who lives in Minnesota and you. I really *do* want us to be sisters, Amy."

Amy felt her eyes sting with tears again, but managed to hold them back. There had already been too much crying today.

"So, will you be my bridesmaid?" Cassie asked.

Amy nodded and the two women hugged.

A door slam and thumping footsteps heralded the entrance of Brock and the boys. "Momma, why are you hugging Auntie Amy?" Zach asked, looking concerned.

Cassie leaned down low and ruffled her son's hair, sending a pang through Amy's heart, just as it always did when she saw mothers interacting with their children. "Auntie Amy is doing me a favor, so I was saying thank you with a nice big hug. She's going to be in the wedding with us," Cassie explained.

Carter's face broke into a wide grin. "We're going to be in the wedding, too! We get to hold the rings and stand next to our uncles!"

Brock held out a hand for each of the boys to high-five. "That's right. Y'all are going to do me proud, I know it."

Carter and Zach both puffed with pleasure.

"So I know now's not the time, what with your imminent date and all," Cassie said, turning back to Amy, "but we need to get you fitted for your bridesmaid dress soon so there'll be time to alter it before the wedding. We're less than a month away at this point."

Amy nodded, taking her role as bridesmaid very

seriously. "I'll be here for whatever you need," she said earnestly.

Brock cut into the sweet, sisterly moment. "Wait, you have a date? With who?" he asked, sounding almost protective.

Cassie gave Amy a worried look, as if she was waiting to see if she'd already slipped up as a sister and confidante. Amy gave her brother a steely gaze. "I'm going on a date with Jack Stuart, and you are not to say anything overprotective or big-brotherly about it."

Brock held up his hands in mock surrender. "I wouldn't think of it. Have fun, my adult sister who can make her own decisions."

Amy and Cassie both smiled in relief.

"But if he tries to get fresh with you—" he began, pointing a finger in warning.

He was cut off when Cassie shoved him out the door. "Sorry about that," Cassie said, grimacing.

Amy laughed. She'd forgotten what it was like to have a big brother around watching out for her. It was a little obnoxious, sure, but also nice in its own way.

"So, let's talk about the wedding," she said, filling the silence.

Cassie shook her head. "Nuh-uh. We're not done here. Next is makeup and hair."

Amy twirled a strand of her blond hair around one of her fingers as she was dragged into the bathroom. "How do you know how to do all this stuff?" she asked.

She'd assumed her doctor sister-in-law was just as clueless as she was, but it seemed very clear that she was wrong. Cassie shrugged as she opened a drawer of brushes and powders. "I have a sister. This is what you do when you're bored over summer vacation."

Amy had never felt like she'd missed out having only brothers, but now she wondered what it would've been like to grow up with a sister. She couldn't go back and change her childhood, but maybe she'd be able to have the closeness of a female sibling now, as an adult. The thought made her smile as she closed her eyes so Cassie could apply eye shadow.

JACK WALKED TO the door of the McNeals' ranch house, a combination of nervousness and excitement turning his stomach into knots. He could well remember being seventeen and feeling that same emotion as he stood waiting for Amy. That was on the occasion of their true first date, when he had nearly convinced himself that it was all a hallucination or something. Or a cruel prank.

It was funny how history repeated itself, he thought as he quelled the sudden voice insisting Amy wouldn't be home. What if she'd changed her mind and taken off again, leaving him without explanation for another decade?

Jack took a deep breath and knocked on the door. It opened almost instantaneously, and he breathed a secret sigh of relief. Amy stood there in all her glory and then some.

"You look…" he began, but words failed him as he took in the sight of her.

Amy's long blond hair cascaded over her shoulders in wavy curls, and her dress was a blue that made her eyes sparkle. Or maybe they were sparkling because she was looking at him.

A man could hope.

When his eyes landed on her scuffed cowboy boots, his expression broke into a wide grin. "My girl knows how to dress for a night out on the town, that's for sure," he commented, chuckling.

For just a split second, Amy's smile faltered and Jack wanted to smack himself. He'd forgotten that this wasn't a decade ago, and Amy wasn't his girl anymore. But then the moment was gone and they were just two strangers standing awkwardly, unsure what came next.

"Is this okay? Since I wasn't sure where we were going, I didn't know how to dress," Amy said as she stepped out onto the porch and closed the front door behind her.

The old Amy would have put some attitude behind the words, teasing Jack for his insistence on making even the most mundane outings a surprise. This time, however, it was just an explanation, nothing more. "You look perfect," he said, earning him another nervous smile.

Jack suddenly felt like this date was a bad idea. She had always been feisty to the point of exasperation, and even a simple compliment rarely went unchallenged. Now she seemed timid, nervous, and he panicked at the thought that she had changed so much and he would forever lose the perfect picture of her he had in his mind. He told himself this was just a strange moment, and they were both acting a little odd because of it.

After waiting all day filled with too much energy,

Jack was already exhausted trying to live each moment in the present and the past.

He made a declaration then and there to give up the constant comparisons. Tonight was about having a nice first date with a beautiful woman.

As if to prove it to himself, he held out his hand to shake hers. "Nice to see you again, Miss Amelia. Thank you for agreeing to go out with me. I know many women would hesitate at a date with a stranger, but I'm sure glad you accepted my offer."

The light in Amy's eye sparkled, and she put on a really terrible Southern Belle accent. "Well, I do declare that it was a might unbecoming of me to allow your advances while I was unchaperoned, but a girl of my age must defy the rules on occasion or she may live the rest of her days as an old spinster."

Jack tried to keep a straight face, but he was wildly unsuccessful, and soon they were both laughing.

"I seem to have come to the wrong house. I was picking up Amy McNeal, not Scarlett O'Hara," he finally managed once the bout of laughter had passed.

"Well, I have never been so insulted in my life!" Scarlett-Amy exclaimed, putting her hand to her heart so dramatically that it sent them both back into giggles.

Jack felt relief course through him. Some things had changed, certainly, but she was still Amy.

They walked down the porch steps, still chuckling, and Jack had to restrain himself from wrapping his arm around her and pulling her in for a kiss. If she wasn't ready yet to be "his girl" again, she probably wasn't ready for a make-out session in the driveway.

To be fair, he wasn't sure if he was ready for that, either. The flood of feelings just being near Amy was almost overwhelming; kissing her could send him right over the edge.

Instead, Jack rushed to the passenger side of his truck and opened the door for her, bowing slightly as he did so. She bobbed her head in appreciation and settled into the seat as he walked around to the driver's side.

"So, where are we going?" she asked the moment he was inside the vehicle.

Jack shook his head. "So impatient," he commented, starting up the vehicle.

"I was once trapped for three days in a shack in India during a monsoon so I could meet an ascetic monk for an article, only to be told that the weather was a bad omen and he refused to speak with me. I'm plenty patient. I just want to know where we're going."

Jack shook his head, not swayed by her story in the least. He turned his truck down the drive and pulled out onto the road. When she settled back in the seat looking resigned, Jack smiled. "You must've had some pretty amazing escapades out there in the world," he said.

Amy nodded. "It's been an adventure. Lonely, though," she said, the last part quiet, as if she was speaking to herself.

Jack knew what that was like. Out on the circuit, there were times when he felt detached from every important thing in his life. His brother, his mom, his home, the town he grew up in. And Amy. Always Amy.

As if she could read the direction of his thoughts, Amy asked, "Are you taking some time off from the circuit right now?"

Jack shrugged. "Involuntarily. My partner broke his leg at our last rodeo. He's decided to take it as a sign that his rodeo days are over, so right now I don't have anyone to ride with. Can't compete in team roping competitions without a partner," he explained.

Amy nodded her understanding. "Well, maybe it's for the best. I imagine there are plenty of people willing to ride with you, and Chester didn't seem all that hot anyway."

Jack was about to tell her that finding a new partner wasn't going to be quite that easy when something she'd said made him pause. How did she know he rode with a guy named Chester? They'd only been competing together for a few years. A glance in her direction made it clear that she'd realized the same thing.

"I keep up with the circuit online," she confessed.

"Including the team sports, huh?" he said, trying to make her blush an even deeper shade of red.

He succeeded, and she didn't need to answer with words—her expression said enough.

So she's been keeping track of me, he thought, feeling a little smug for just a moment, until he realized he wasn't exactly being fair. He knew he would need to tell her his own little secret.

"I read your articles, you know," he said. "Every one. I have for years. I even learned how to set up a filter so anything with your byline goes straight to my email."

He knew she was staring at him, but he couldn't bring himself to turn his eyes from the road in front of him. He didn't want her to know everything he was sure his eyes would say.

Luckily, they soon pulled up in front of Tony's Steak House at exactly the right moment. "I hope you're not a vegetarian or anything," he said as he parked the truck.

"No matter how much I've traveled, I'm still from Texas," she answered, as if that obviously settled the question.

Jack went around and opened Amy's door for her, but decided not to try to take her hand. Even after their giggles and confessions, she still seemed ill-at-ease. But that was fine—there would be plenty of time for that later. He hoped.

For now, it was enough to be walking with her into the "fancy" restaurant that a teenage version of himself had taken Amy to for her eighteenth birthday after scrimping and saving for months in order to be able to afford it.

"It's been a long time," she said, as if he'd mentioned that romantic dinner they'd had so long ago.

"It's not going to break the bank for us to eat here this time," he answered, though that might not be entirely true if he couldn't find a new roping partner soon.

"I remember I was too nervous to order anything on the menu because I thought it would bankrupt you. You had to finally order for me just so I wouldn't have a meal of table bread and water." Amy smiled at the memory.

Jack could remember every moment of that evening they'd had together, and the images it brought to mind sent zings of pleasure through him. If he wanted to go slow with Amy, start from zero, a walk down memory lane certainly wasn't going to help.

"I really wanted to impress the beautiful stranger tonight, so I thought this would be the best place to take her. It may not be the Ritz, but it has great steaks and happens to be the nicest restaurant within a fifty-mile radius."

"I bet you take all your dates here," Amy commented, playing along.

"Only the most interesting ones. And never on a first date. I'm not *made* of money."

She chuckled. "I guess neither of us are pulling in the big bucks, huh? Weekly dates here are still just a dream."

He remembered the "one day" conversation they'd had shortly after the birthday dinner, talking about when they'd have enough money to eat there all the time, after he'd become a star on the rodeo circuit. Teenagers with big hopes and very little real-world experience.

For Amy, though, he'd gladly take her to Tony's for every meal until he went broke, if it made her happy.

They stepped inside the dim, romantic atmosphere of the restaurant and were quickly seated in a small corner booth. He took off his cowboy hat and slipped it onto a hat peg before holding her chair out for her.

They settled in at their table, the candlelight flickering on the table.

After they looked at their menus for a few moments, Jack asked one of the many questions he'd been wondering about since he'd heard she was in town. "So, what made you decide to come to Spring Valley for a month-long visit when you haven't been home for that long in a decade?"

He tried to say it in a conversational tone, but he doubted it hid how curious he was in the answer.

"I thought we were doing the 'beautiful stranger' thing," Amy told him.

She sounded almost nervous, but Jack had to know. "How about we each get one nonstranger question?"

Amy sighed and looked at her water glass as if she suddenly found condensation to be very interesting. She was quiet for a moment, like she was gathering her thoughts. He waited, eager to hear what had changed.

"I was robbed at gunpoint about a month ago," she said.

"Someone pulled a gun on you?" he responded, shocked.

"Shh," she whispered urgently, ducking her head a little at his outburst.

It took Jack a second to realize how loud he'd been. Of everything he'd expected her to say, that hadn't been it.

"Someone pulled a gun on you?" he repeated, much quieter this time.

Amy shrugged. "I was walking around the Medina in Morocco at night and got pulled into an abandoned alley. It's fine," she added, placing a calming hand on his arm. "I wasn't hurt or anything, and all they got was a little bit of cash and my phone. Still, it was unnerving. I was in a bad place mentally for a while."

She paused, and Jack waited. It seemed like she was making some sort of decision, though what it could be, he had no idea. "Eventually I realized I needed to come home, see my family. And settle some unfinished business," she finished, her face grim.

He pointed to himself to check that she meant he was the unfinished business.

"Yes, you. And—you know, this is going way deeper than first-date conversations usually do," she said.

He was leaning forward with interest. What else could she possibly have left undone that would be changed by a near-death experience?

"And?" he prompted.

"And I figured I should meet my half sister. She emailed me a few months back, but I hadn't responded. I didn't know what to say. It took that gun pressed to my head to get me to realize I wanted to meet her. We're going to see each other next week."

Jack let out a low whistle and sat back. He'd always known Amy was adopted, but she'd never seemed curious about her biological family. The McNeals were enough, she used to say.

Before either of them could say anything else, their server arrived, and the moment she'd left with the orders—two steaks, of course—Amy turned to him.

"Okay, I answered your one non-first-date question. Now it's my turn."

"Fire away," he said, wondering what on earth she might want to ask.

Chapter Four

Amy looked into Jack's eyes as he waited for whatever question she might throw at him, an open book. Guilt rushed through her.

She should have told him about what else had happened after the robbery, about Armand and the last push that finally sent her home to him, to this date. She just hadn't been able to make herself say it. Telling Cassie was one thing, but this was Jack. For the time being, Amy couldn't say the words aloud, see his reaction, feel the shame all over again.

"You okay?" Jack asked, putting his hand over hers. "You can ask me anything, Ames," he said, trying to reassure her.

Amy looked at Jack and resolved to tell him about Armand another time. For now, she wanted to have an enjoyable date with a man who was sweet and honest.

There was one question she could ask that might assuage her guilt a little, though, and she grasped at that straw. "What's your dating life been like since I left?" she asked, hoping to get answers to her real questions.

Did you forget about me? Have you loved others, even for a short time, since I've been gone?

She wouldn't have been able to say what answer she wanted to hear, but she had to know.

Jack gave her a little smile she couldn't interpret. "I've dated a few women here and there," he said.

Amy wasn't sure what to do with that, but before she could say anything he continued. "Nobody ever quite met the bar you set, so none of them lasted long. I think they knew as well as I did that there was always someone's shadow between us."

His blue eyes gazed into hers, and Amy felt gratitude and pain rush through her. She grasped his hand tightly, assuring herself that he was real, not just some wistful daydream. He squeezed back.

After a short silence, Amy let go and cleared her throat. This was getting too intimate for her comfort, and she decided it was best to change topics. "Do you have any prospects for your next roping partner?" she asked.

This set off a lively conversation of prospective candidates, and since Amy was, as she had confessed in the truck, up-to-date on the current competitors in Jack's field, they were able to both contribute to the discussion. They talked about it through dinner, between ordering food and being served their meals.

When the waiter cleared the dishes and they wrapped up rodeo talk, Jack asked, "Tell me more about what you've been up to, Ames. Is hotfooting it around the world as wonderful as you make it out to be in your articles? It always seems like even the disasters are once-in-a-lifetime adventures."

Amy ran a finger through the condensation on her water glass as she thought about what to share. Armand's face popped up once more, but she shoved it back down. Still not the right time. "It's not always as glamorous and fun as my writing suggests, no. Getting up at 4:00 a.m. when you're still jet-lagged because you need to move on to the next thing, even though you've hardly seen any of the cool new city you landed in two days ago, or typing on a laptop while sitting next to a toilet in a sketchy *alburgue* because you have a deadline and it doesn't care that you have food poisoning, or discovering that you were a few hundred yards away from a bombing in Istanbul. Having a strange man hold a gun to my head and shout in a language I don't understand."

A smooth talker getting what he wants from you, making you care for him, and then treating you like trash, she added silently. Amy cleared her throat, refusing to allow the tears stinging her eyes to fall. "Situations like that have made me wonder why the hell I'm not curled up in my bed with a book while Ma makes me a delicious meal," she finished.

Jack looked at her curiously, and she waited for the question she knew would come next. "Then why are you still doing it?"

She shook her head, knowing her answer wasn't going to do her experiences justice. "For every terrifying or awful moment I have, I get dozens of nuggets of perfection. The sun rising over Mount Fuji, or a stranger insisting they help you find your hotel and refusing any payment. A pickup soccer game with kids in South Africa."

It was a little disheartening, though not at all unexpected, for her to see that Jack didn't really understand what she meant. He had never felt wanderlust. Heck, up until she moved away to college, she hadn't, either. They had planned to honeymoon in Vegas to see the National Finals Rodeo and counted that an exotic trip to a far-off land.

Amy smiled at the memory, even though it made her a little sad. She had changed so much since she was a teenager. The past few weeks had made that clear.

Perhaps she'd changed too much to even be here, on this date with Jack. She didn't want to let herself think that through.

Luckily, Jack saved the conversation by picking up the dessert menu. "So, what do you want? The lava cake?"

Amy put a hand over her stomach and groaned. "I ate way too much to be tempted by dessert, and you have to bring up my biggest weakness? That's not fair."

He smiled at her. "How about I share it with you? Half a lava cake isn't too much for anybody."

She readily agreed, and soon they were dipping their spoons into the molten chocolate. Amy closed her eyes as the hot dessert melted on her tongue. "I've tried a million desserts in more countries than I can count, but this beats them all hands down."

"Maybe Texas deserves to be a regular stop for you

from now on, huh? You know, since there's delicious lava cake to be had."

Amy wasn't fooled one bit into thinking Jack wanted her to come home more often because of a dessert, but she looked at the cake anyway. "Maybe I'll need to start making longer visits home a regular thing. For chocolate's sake," she said, glancing up into his eyes.

He gave her a smile that curled her insides and made her wish they were somewhere much more private.

Whatever else was true of the past decade, Amy knew that she had never quite gotten over her high school sweetheart, and here she was so close to him she could feel the heat coming off his skin. She knew she would be a fool to throw that away, no matter what ghosts tailed her.

Soon they were walking out into the brisk autumn air, and Amy only wished the date could have been longer. In fact, she didn't want it to end, to be left alone in her room with her worst thoughts and doubts. With Jack she felt safe, protected.

"I'd like to take you one last place before I drive you home," Jack told her as they settled into his truck.

Amy let out a silent sigh of relief. "Where?" she asked, curious.

"You'll see," he said mysteriously before turning his eyes to the windshield and the road before them.

Jack was always trying to surprise her when they were teens, so it seemed only fitting he would have another trick up his sleeve. Amy settled back and waited, knowing any attempt to learn more about his plan would be futile.

It only took a few minutes for her to realize where they were going, anyway, and a thrill went through her that she forcibly tamped down. He might be driving her to his house, but that probably didn't mean what her body wished it might mean. Even if it did, she knew it was too soon for her to get on that horse again, as much as Jack's presence sent her into overdrive.

"Taking me home to meet your mother? That's a pretty big step for a first date," she said, reminding herself to keep things light and slow.

Jack cocked a smile in her direction. "It's past eight, which means she's already in bed reading one of her mystery novels. A visit with her will need to wait."

Then what was his plan? She couldn't begin to guess, so she sat back and waited as Jack parked his truck in front of Stuart Ranch.

"Come on," Jack said as he opened Amy's door and took her hand, pulling her toward the barn. Amy followed without thinking, her mind focused on their hands. They hadn't made much physical contact throughout the date, and each time was purposely cut short, as if they'd both been avoiding something they knew to be dangerous. But now her hand was wrapped in his, and it felt as if it had never belonged anywhere else. Her heart thumped hard in her chest.

Then they were in the dark barn and Amy was distracted by the familiar sight and smells. She had spent countless hours in that barn with Jack doing all manner of things. Some innocent, but many less so, and those thoughts thrilled her.

Jack pulled her along until they were among the rows of horses, and then he reached up and pulled a cord to a bare bulb, illuminating a small circle around them. Amy looked at Jack, waiting for him to explain what exactly he was thinking, but he said nothing. He just pointed to a nearby stall.

Amy walked over, curious, and what she saw took her breath away. It was Bandit, *her* horse, the one that had died almost ten years ago. The same markings, the same shake of the head. Everything.

"How…" she began, but was unable to formulate her amazement into words.

"This is Maverick, sired by Bandit just after you— Just after we graduated," Jack answered.

She knew what he'd been about to say: *just after you left.* It stung, but she ignored it. The animal walked up to her and pressed his head against her just the way Bandit always had.

Amy could feel tears in her eyes yet again, for joy this time.

JACK WATCHED AMY hug Maverick's neck and knew she was hiding her face so he wouldn't see her cry. Ever since the foal was born, Jack knew Amy would be shocked to see the likeness to Bandit, but for a long while he'd thought she would never have the chance. As soon as she'd agreed to go on a date with him, he knew that this would be an important part of the evening.

Amy leaned back from Maverick's neck and smiled, though her eyes were red. She patted the horse's neck gently. "It looks just like him," she said.

Jack smiled. "I know. Acts like him, too. I've always thought he has his father's spirit."

He didn't say that seeing Maverick every once in a while had helped when he missed her too much. Caring for the animal was, in a way, like caring for a little piece of Amy.

As they stood in silence together beside the horse's stall, a light pitter-patter on the roof told them it had begun to rain.

"Can I come back and see him again?" Amy asked, her voice so quiet Jack almost didn't hear her.

"Of course," Jack told her. "You're always welcome here, no matter what."

With that, she said goodbye to Maverick and they walked to the barn door. For a long minute, they stood watching the rain fall, glittering in the light from his childhood home. It was getting late, and those lights would go out soon.

His mind drifted back to long-ago hidden moments spent in this same barn with this same woman, and the urge to kiss her overwhelmed him. He turned to Amy, and as if she had been anticipating this exact moment, she fell into his arms with an almost desperate urgency.

With their lips together, Jack knew what heaven must be like. The lifting, soaring feeling inside him overshadowed any possible worries about falling in love with Amy all over again. If this kiss was any indication, he'd never managed to recover from the first time, whatever he'd told himself.

After what seemed like several lifetimes, their lips broke apart, though neither of them moved from their embrace. Jack rested his forehead against Amy's and tried to gather all his control for what he knew he should say. "My truck doesn't handle rain well, so I should probably get you home before the rain gets too bad and we're stuck out here," he told her.

"Would that be so bad?" she asked, still breathless from the kiss.

Jack groaned quietly. "If you're *not* suggesting we sleep together, you need to tell me now. I've only got so much self-control, and most of it is being used to have this conversation instead of kiss you again."

In answer, Amy put her hand on the back of Jack's neck and guided his lips back to hers. She seemed to almost be pleading for his attentions, as if she needed him right at that moment, and he could do nothing but oblige. He was sure she could feel his own eagerness for the connection he'd been missing for so long.

Everything about them being together was familiar and comfortable, yet new in surprising ways, and afterward they lay together on a makeshift bed of horse blankets.

Jack wanted to say something, but what was there to say? It had all been said already, everything except *I still love you*, and he wasn't ready to say that yet. The fear that she would leave all over again was still strong inside him.

Amy sat up, and Jack looked at her carefully. She seemed worried. Remorseful, maybe?

"I think the rain's stopped, and it's late," she said.

Jack sat up, too. Was that really how they were going to end this night—it's getting late, see you later? It seemed that she regretted how quickly things had progressed now that it was over, and the thought sent a pang through his heart.

After all, to him they were just continuing from where they'd been a decade ago, however much he tried to pretend this was a first date. He couldn't regret one bit of what they'd done, except if it hurt her, somehow.

They gathered their clothes in silence and dressed, then made their way through the inky darkness to his truck. Once they started on the road, though, Jack knew their night couldn't end like this. He wanted her to know that he didn't consider what had happened as just some fling in the barn. He may still have lingering worries about her disappearing again, but that wasn't going to stop him from pursuing some sort of relationship with her.

"What are you doing tomorrow? I was thinking we could take Maverick out for a ride. Maybe you can help me practice my roping skills if you're up for it. I need to keep sharp if I'm going to find a good partner," he said.

"I haven't competed in so long," Amy said wistfully.

"You were wonderful, you know. And some things are like riding a bike," he told her, only partly talking about horse-riding.

"That's true," she answered in a quiet murmur, and he saw out of the corner of his eye that she was smiling, but it didn't completely erase the lines of worry on her forehead. He wished that he could read her thoughts.

"I'm sure Ma has a big Sunday dinner thing planned for tomorrow," she said.

"Celebrating the prodigal daughter's return?" Jack asked, trying not to be too disappointed.

"Something like that," Amy responded. "Jose and Diego will be coming into town and everything."

Before Jack could suggest another time to meet, Amy added, "But I can be free for a while in the morning, if that's okay," saying it all in a rush, as if it was against her better judgment.

"Sounds great," he answered quickly, in case she might try to take back what she'd said.

He was already looking forward to the time when they'd see each other again.

AMY LAY IN bed later that night, staring at the ceiling, berating herself over all the rash decisions she'd made that evening and wishing she could go back and change them. She knew, though, that if she had the chance, she would do it all again. Her skin still tingled from Jack's touch.

Even though it was past two in the morning, Amy felt wide-awake. There were too many thoughts swirling around in her head for her to even consider sleeping. Was she just going to pick things up with Jack right where they left off a decade ago, despite everything that had changed? Is that what he wanted? Is that what *she* wanted? Even if it was, would that be enough?

She knew they shouldn't have slept together so soon, while Armand's shadow still loomed so strongly. Still, she couldn't regret it. Jack was such a comforting presence, and her body had begged for comfort. His touch erased some of the shame and guilt she'd felt the past few days, even if it added a little more in the process. After all, he deserved to know everything about her last few weeks in Morocco before she jumped into bed with him. And she resolved to not let it happen again until they had a long, honest conversation.

Finally Amy couldn't take it anymore. She needed to talk out her thoughts, and she knew who she needed to turn to for guidance.

"Morning, Queen Bee," Amy said softly as the horse snorted a greeting to her.

Amy felt a little bad about turning on the barn's light and disturbing the horses trying to sleep, but she needed to speak her mind or she'd go crazy.

Luckily, Queen Bee seemed to understand, because she nuzzled Amy's shoulder affectionately. Amy stroked the animal's neck, feeling comforted. This animal seemed like just the one to listen to the thoughts bouncing around in her brain. "I'm feeling lost right now, Q.B.," Amy started. "I just want to put Armand behind me and enjoy my time here, but I can't seem to. Not yet, anyway. And now there's so much to consider about Jack and me. I mean, I don't know what I want for us, or what's even feasible. Closure? A fresh start? To pick things up where we left off? It's...confusing, to say the least."

Queen Bee tossed her head. "You agree, huh?" Amy said, hugging the horse's neck. "If we try to start a relationship, is it just going to be a do-over of our past? I'm not sure that's even possible, with all that's happened. I've changed too much for that, I think. Or maybe I haven't, you know? Do I really *need* to hop on planes all the time to make a few bucks? I'm sure I could find a job writing articles right here in Spring Valley."

The large animal tossed her head again and snorted. Amy nodded. "You're right. I'd go crazy staying in Spring Valley for the rest of my life. Heck, I've only been here for two days and already I'm having conversations with horses. As much as I love it here, I'd probably go all *Yellow Wallpaper* in a few months."

Queen Bee tilted her head and stared at Amy, who gave an exaggerated sigh. "It's a story, Q.B. A famous one. Really, you should read more literature."

Amy laughed and sat down on a bench across from Queen Bee's stall. "I can't tell you how glad I am that you're a horse and can't tell anyone how insane I am, Q.B."

"Yeah, but if one of your brothers happened to drive home in the middle of the night and go out to the barn to investigate the light on there, you could be in trouble," a voice said from behind Amy, nearly giving her a heart attack.

She stood and spun to find one of her twin brothers standing not ten feet from her. "Diego, you scared me!" she admonished.

Even though her brothers were identical twins, she was sure she was speaking to Diego. Jose would have come roaring in with a big grin and a teasing laugh, not the quiet smile and kind eyes Diego always employed. As if to reinforce the difference, Diego sat beside his adopted sister and wrapped an arm around her. "Just be glad Jose's not showing up until midday tomorrow. He would have teased you mercilessly, then told everyone, just to round things out nicely."

Amy put her head on Diego's shoulder. "Yeah, he would. Thanks for not being a jackass."

Diego shrugged. "He's just getting through life the best way he knows how. Things haven't always been easy for him, you know."

Amy nodded, though her mind wasn't able to focus much on Jose and his problems, which she frankly doubted even existed. He was always the joker, the funny man. The life of every party, flitting from one thing to the next with the good luck of the lighthearted and carefree. She couldn't imagine what types of problems he could possibly have.

"So, do you want to talk about it?" Diego asked after a minute of silence.

"It depends. How much did you hear?"

"Not much, just the part about you going crazy if you move here for good. Is that suddenly a possibility?"

"Well," Amy started, not sure what her answer would be. "No, it's not. One date with my high school sweetheart can't change who I am—"

"You mean Jack Stuart?" Diego cut in, sounding surprised. "Are you two getting back together?"

Amy had forgotten that Diego and Jose, being a year younger, had still been home during her senior year. Diego at least was observant enough to notice how serious their relationship had been.

Amy put her head in her hands. "That's just it. I don't know. We only had one date, but it already feels serious, and I'm not ready for that."

There's still so much unsaid between us, she thought.

Diego squeezed her shoulders. "Hey, you don't need to make any big decisions if you don't want to. Just because you two dated a decade ago doesn't mean you have to start at square ten instead of square one."

Amy nodded. She knew all that, and Jack had said the same thing. So why was her mind insisting she make it so significant?

Because it didn't *feel* like they were at square one. Certainly not after what had happened between them just a few hours before.

But that didn't mean she couldn't slow things down and enjoy whatever it was they had without putting a label on it.

"Thanks, Diego," Amy said, standing. "I better get to bed. Jack and I are going to go riding in the morning."

Diego stood, too. "Just do me one favor—if you need advice, avoid getting it from horses. They're all a bunch of neigh-sayers," he said, giving Amy a big smile at his terrible pun.

Amy rolled her eyes. "Maybe you should leave the jokes to Jose."

Diego shrugged. "Fair enough."

Together they walked to the house to get some much-needed sleep.

Chapter Five

The next morning, Jack awoke at the crack of dawn, excited to spend the morning with Amy even though he'd brought her home past midnight and he wasn't expecting her to arrive for at least three hours.

Everyone else in the house was still asleep, enjoying their long, restful Sunday morning, so Jack crept quietly out of the house and down to the barn. Once there, he groomed Maverick until his coat shone, talking to him all the while. "Okay, boy, you treat Amy right, you hear? She's special, and I expect you to be on your best behavior."

Maverick tossed his head impatiently, and Jack chuckled. "Fine, fine. You know what to do. I'll stop beating a dead…well, you know," he finished, trying to spare the animal the insensitive idiom.

"Oh, and last thing," Jack said, looking Maverick straight in the eye. "Don't let her know I spend so much time talking to horses. I don't want her to think I've gone crazy since high school."

Maverick dipped his head in what was an unmistakable nod and Jack patted his neck. "Thanks, boy," he said.

Once Maverick and Benny, Jack's favorite horse, were ready for riding, Jack went about the other chores of the ranch, desperate to keep himself occupied until Amy arrived. He mucked out the stalls, despite the thorough cleaning he'd given them the day before, fed the horses and prepared the paddock for roping practice.

After everything was done to perfection, Jack glanced at the time on his phone and groaned. It had hardly passed seven thirty in the morning.

What was he supposed to do for the next hour and a half? If he kept up at this pace, soon he would need to start breaking things around the ranch just so he'd have something to fix while he waited for Amy.

Even though it was a cool morning, Jack could feel sweat drying on the back of his neck, smell hay and horse on his skin, and he brightened a little. At least it was still early enough that he could take a shower before seeing Amy.

Jack went inside through the kitchen door of the old ranch house intending to cut through to the bathroom, only to find his brother Tom at the stove.

"I didn't figure you'd be out and about yet," Jack commented.

Tom seemed just as surprised. "What've you been up to so early this morning?"

Jack shrugged, trying to seem cool and relaxed. "Amy's coming over for some roping practice, so I was getting everything ready."

Tom seemed about to ask more questions, but then apparently decided against it and went back to cooking. Jack was grateful to have his brother's penetrating gaze off him. "Well, I'm making plenty of food, so sit and have something. And after that, since you're up so early, you can help me muck stalls."

"Already done," Jack said, earning another curious glance from his brother. "What? I couldn't sleep, so I thought it would be nice to take care of a few things around here. You don't always need to be on the hook for everything."

Unfortunately, Tom didn't take the bait. He just raised his eyebrow further. "It's just surprising you have so much energy this morning, after how late you got home last night. That must've been some date."

Jack blushed a little and picked up his fork as Tom set a plate of eggs in front of him. "It went well," he said, trying not to picture the escapade in the barn in case Tom also acquired mind-reading abilities when he became so insightful and learned how to cook.

"Well," Tom said, sighing, "I'm happy you're having a good time."

Jack looked at his brother as he chewed his breakfast. When, exactly, did Tom stop being happy? Was it when he took over the ranch duties and started to see the bills stacking up, or when their dad died a year ago? Or had he gone sour even before then?

Whichever it was, Jack knew he should talk to his brother and try to find a way to make his life better. He'd sacrificed so much so Jack could live his life on the circuit and their mom could stay put on the ranch she'd owned her entire adult life.

Jack looked at his phone and cursed quietly. If he hoped to get a shower before Amy arrived, a heart-to-heart with Tom would need to wait. Under the time display was a new text from Amy:

Hope it's okay if I head over now. Excited to try my hand at roping again!

Jack sent her a quick reply and rushed off to the shower, leaving Tom alone at the table, smiling slightly at his older brother's disappearing form and determined to speak with him soon.

Washed and dressed, Jack hurried into the living room just as a truck pulled into the driveway. He didn't recognize the vehicle, but he certainly recognized the driver. Amy, her hair tied back and her cowboy hat on her head, looked as lovely as ever.

She may not feel like she belongs here, he thought, *but she is Texas through and through.*

AMY STEPPED OUT of Diego's truck carefully and looked up to see Jack standing in the front window of the sprawling ranch house, watching her. Her stomach gave a twist of excitement.

Despite the lack of sleep, she'd woken up early, unable to rest when she knew she'd be seeing Jack again so soon. She'd waited as long as she could until, feeling too impatient to wait any longer, she asked to borrow Diego's keys. He handed them over with nothing more

than a smile and a reminder to be home by noon or
face the wrath of Ma, and she was once again grateful
that Diego, not Jose, had been the one to come home
during the night.

Jack opened the door as she walked up the steps,
and Amy could see he had just showered. He probably had to rush into the shower when she sent her
text, and she wished she'd been more patient. Heck,
she might've even woken him up. It was Sunday morning, after all, and they'd been up late the night before.
"Sorry about getting here so early," she began, but he
waved her apology aside.

"I've been up for a while," he said, running a hand
through his damp hair. "Just needed a quick rinse after
mucking out the stalls."

Amy made a face. She'd done that job enough times
to know that a rinse afterward was more than welcome.
He nodded his agreement and ushered her into the
house. Amy looked around the living room, with its an-
tique furniture and flowered wallpaper, and for a moment she felt seventeen again, coming over to visit with
Jack and his family right after they'd started dating.

"Not much changes around here, huh?" Jack said,
following her gaze.

Amy nodded but couldn't find the right words to
say. She felt panic rise in her for a moment before
she reminded herself that an unchanged living room
couldn't suddenly suck her into the past, where she
and Jack were practically engaged.

Luckily, Jack's brother walked in, and the erased
years came flying back. He looked more than a de-

cade older, careworn, with an air of anxiety about him. He smiled and held out his hand, grasping hers tight. "Amy. It's so good to see you. Would you like some breakfast?"

Before she could politely decline, her stomach grumbled. Tom nodded. "I'll take that as a yes," he said, leading her into the kitchen.

She and Jack sat beside each other at the table as Tom fixed her a plate of eggs and sausage. Jack already had a plate still half-filled with food, but he waited until she had her own before he resumed eating.

Amy put a forkful in her mouth and savored the flavor of eggs, bell peppers and cheese. If nothing else, Texas had great food.

As she ate, Amy kept her eyes on Tom—her conflicting feelings about Jack made Tom a much easier target for her attention, and his behavior gave her something to think about. While perfectly warm and friendly, he also seemed distant in a way. As if his thoughts were somewhere else.

"So Tom," she said, breaking the silence. "It's been a long time since I've seen you. What are you up to these days?"

Even though neither of the men moved, Amy could feel a shift in the air, as if they'd both stiffened.

"Not much. Just taking care of the ranch," he said.

Amy was no expert, but that didn't sound like his idea of a dream job from the way he said it.

"How about you? Brock told me you've been traveling all over the world," Tom said.

Amy nodded, forcing herself not to slide her gaze

over to Jack. Did he and his brother ever talk about anything? If he was hearing about stuff like that from Brock, it seemed not.

Though maybe she'd been such a sore spot in Jack's life that he didn't talk about her. That thought brought with it the sour feeling of guilt, and she turned her attention back to Tom.

"Yes, I write for some different websites and magazines. Have you traveled much?"

Tom leaned back and sighed. "I did a fair amount back in college, but not lately."

She could hear the wistfulness in his voice. It seemed clear he was itching to get away from this ranch, do something other than run the riding school his parents started. Amy could empathize.

Before she could ask another question, Tom stood and gathered the empty plates. "Well, you two have fun today. I'll be working on paperwork a good part of the morning, so you'll have the run of the ranch."

With that, he disappeared, leaving Amy and Jack alone. They stood, Jack opened the back door and together they walked toward the barn, the scene of so many intimacies, old and new. As they walked, Jack said quietly, "He doesn't seem very happy, does he?"

Amy shook her head. "Any idea why?"

Jack sighed. "I think it's mostly the financial shape the ranch is in. We're pretty strapped right now and it worries him. He thinks everything's his responsibility."

Amy thought about what Jack said. That was probably a big problem for him, but she had a feeling there was something else to it. Still, she had to assume Jack knew more about it then she did. "Is the plan still for you to take over the ranch and turn it into a rodeo school?"

Jack nodded. "Spring Valley could use it, if I could just get the money together to make it happen. Tom wants to go off and do something else, I know, but until I land a few big wins, I don't know how to make any of that happen."

"What does Tom want to do when he leaves the ranch?" Amy asked.

"I'm not really sure, but he definitely doesn't want to be here. I know that much," Jack said shrugging.

They had stepped inside the shade of the barn at this point, and Amy leaned against the wall and crossed her arms, thinking about their predicament. "What does your mother think about the situation?"

Jack looked a little embarrassed. "I don't think she knows much about it, to tell the truth. Tom keeps it quiet so she doesn't worry."

"Your mother doesn't know the ranch is struggling and her son isn't happy?" Amy asked, surprised.

Jack gave her a sad shake of his head. "Mom's lived here for almost forty years. And she's getting older. We don't want her to be burdened with all that."

"It seems to me she deserves to know the truth about what's going on. And maybe if the three of you sat down and discussed some things, you could find a way to make everyone happy."

"I don't think it's going to be that easy," Jack said as he moved toward the stalls holding Benny and Maverick.

"At least it would open a dialogue and give her the chance to give her opinions. I know your mom—she's a smart woman."

Amy watched Jack seem to consider this, and then he nodded. "You're right. She deserves to know what's going on."

Amy felt relief. For some reason, helping the Stuarts figure out their difficulties made her feel like she might just be able to figure out her own.

Jack brought Maverick to her and Amy began saddling the horse, running her hands through his coat as she cinched the belt tight beneath him. He was so much like Bandit it made her heart skip.

"Now, on the topic of siblings, let's talk about yours. You have a sister?" Jack asked as he saddled his own horse.

Amy hadn't been expecting the topic to come up and took a moment to gather her thoughts. She still wasn't sure how she felt about the whole thing and hadn't talked to anyone else about it, so she didn't know what to say. "A younger half sister. Different fathers. Her name's Maryanne. She lives in California, but she's flying in to Austin and we agreed to meet for lunch there this Wednesday."

"Are you excited meet some of your biological family?" Jack asked as they both mounted their horses.

Amy had no real answer. Her whole life, Ma and Pop, Brock, Diego and Jose had always been plenty of family. As loving as anyone could want. What if her new sibling wasn't as wonderful as her adopted family?

And what if she was?

Jack seemed to realize she was struggling to respond to his question, because he turned his horse toward the barn doors. "How about we do some riding
and talk about this stuff later? Benny is chomping at
the bit to get some exercise."

Amy followed, glad for the reprieve.

Soon they were out in the cool fall sunshine, and
Amy breathed in the autumn air. It smelled like rain
and grass and animals, somehow distinctly Texas. It
was a smell she hadn't even realized she missed in the
deserts of Africa.

Soon they were riding at a trot through the familiar trails around the ranch, warming up the horses. It
should have also been a chance for Amy and Maverick
to become familiar with one another, but that wasn't
really necessary. To Amy, it was like she and Maverick were old friends.

She took a deep breath, put away any worries she
had about the next few days and weeks, and focused
her attention on enjoying herself in this perfect moment.

JACK GLANCED BACK at Amy and felt his heart lift at the
sight of her. She was sitting with her head thrown back,
as if she was breathing in all of Texas. She looked so
relaxed and comfortable riding on Maverick. Happy.

It was the same look he'd glimpsed a few times the
night before when it had been just the two of them in
the barn.

Benny shook his head and nickered, as if to remind
Jack to stay in the here and now, and Jack turned his

attention to the trail in front of them, patting the animal on the neck to show he got the message.

At that moment, Amy rode up beside him. "Should we get back to the paddock and do some roping before it gets too late?" she asked as Maverick and Benny matched strides.

Before Amy had arrived that morning, Jack had felt like he had the entire day before him, but now that she was here it seemed to be quickly disappearing. He nodded in agreement and together they turned the animals back toward the paddocks nearest the barn.

"Don't judge me if I'm terrible," Amy warned him. "I haven't lassoed anything in years."

"I'm sure you'll pick it back up soon enough," Jack assured her.

He'd never been longer than a week without a rope in his hand for as far back as he could remember, and he couldn't even guess what it would be like to be so long out of practice. Roping was just something he did, a consistent part of his life, and he hoped Amy would remember how much she loved roping, too.

He tried not to acknowledge the part of him wishing she would remember all the things she used to love here in Texas, including him, and that maybe if she did, she wouldn't want to leave. The idea that an hour or two of rodeo exercises would make Amy give up her life and settle back in Spring Valley seemed crazy, he knew, but he couldn't stop himself from hoping.

In the ring, he gathered ropes from where he'd hung them on the fence and tossed one to Amy, keeping one for himself. He moved to the opposite end of the paddock to give them space to practice. "Do you want to dismount?" he asked, wondering if she was so rusty that lassoing while on top of a horse might seem intimidating.

In true Amy fashion, she looked at him with raised eyebrows and gave a sarcastic snort. "The day I can't handle a rope from the back of a horse is still a long way off yet, Jack."

Jack noticed with some amusement that her cowgirl twang, which had gone subtle over time, had grown in intensity now that she had a lasso in her hand.

Soon they were both working with the ropes, swinging them in wide circles over their heads and tossing them over various posts, tightening as the loop dropped over the target. This was child's play for Jack, a professional roper, but he thought it might be best for Amy to start with something simple. It quickly became apparent, however, that he had been right about roping being like riding a bike.

In no time at all, Amy was racing around the paddock on Maverick, roping her targets at high speeds and adding to the difficulty by aiming for more distant posts and turning Maverick at the last second, making the tosses more elaborate as her muscle memory took over. Soon, her face was flushed and she was giving Jack a wide grin.

"Not bad," he commented.

Amy rolled her eyes. "Not bad? I've still got it, Jack! Heck, I could give you a run for your money."

Jack shook his head, more to annoy her than anything else. "I'm going easy right now. Don't want to embarrass you with my superior skills."

Amy gave him a skeptical look, then blew a strand of hair back from her face. Jack urged Benny close to her and tucked the strand behind her ear. "You're fantastic, Amy," he said quietly, his hand lingering for an extra second on her cheek before he pulled it away.

She moved away, and although she tried to seem nonchalant, there was a hint of panic on her face. Had he moved too quickly, been too intimate for her comfort? That seemed odd considering what had happened between them the night before, but he couldn't deny her discomfort, and it cut at him.

For a brief moment there, he'd felt as if there was nothing between them, no past hurts or missing years. Now all that rushed back in, reminding him oh-so-clearly that this couldn't possibly be that easy. Jack prayed Amy wouldn't disappear from his life again before he had a chance to break through some of those walls. She truly was fantastic, in so many ways besides her lassoing skills, and he was sure life without her in it would go back to that grey, lonely place it had been for months after she'd left the first time. But this time, he might not ever find his way back. He was too old to fall out of love with her now.

Jack turned away from her and steered Benny toward the far end of the paddock. "Since we're warmed up, how about we try some team exercises?" Jack called over his shoulder.

He was answered with a clatter of hooves as Maverick galloped to catch up to him and Benny. Together,

Jack and Amy surveyed the paddock and the dummy steer Jack had hauled out of the barn that morning. "No real stock to work with?" Amy asked.

Jack shook his head. "Not until I can get my rodeo school going," he said. "The closest place for real rodeo practice is an hour away. I know if I can pull together the money, it'll be profitable. There are so many rodeo hopefuls around here that could really use the opportunity to improve." Then, realizing he'd gotten off topic, he refocused on the dummy fifty feet away. "You want to take the header position?" he asked.

Amy seemed to consider a moment before nodding. "Sure, no pressure. Just roping my first steer in a decade with a pro as my teammate."

Jack laughed and leaned in for a quick peck on her cheek before moving away to give her room. If she was nervous, it didn't show, and she called and lassoed like a pro. They caught the dummy smoothly, their timing nearly perfect. Amy gave him a satisfied smile as she pulled her rope from around the horn and nose of the steer. "Not top marks, and it *is* a fake animal, but still, that wasn't bad."

Jack agreed. "Not bad at all. Should we try again?"

The second time around, they did even better, Amy's lasso falling squarely over the steer's horns. The third, her throw was long and missed the dummy completely. Even though Jack could see that Amy was getting sore and tired, she insisted on continuing and they went through the workout another five times, until Amy's throw was so bad that they both sagged on their horses in laughter.

"Were you trying to lasso the dummy, or me?" Jack asked, his eyes sparkling with amusement.

"If I was trying to get you, it was purely my subconscious. While there's a lot to be said for muscle memory, it seems being in shape is fairly important, too. My arm feels like a wet noodle."

Jack looked up at the sun. "It's probably best we stop now, anyway, if you don't want your ma in a tizzy."

They dismounted and walked the horses into the barn, and then brushed them down side by side in comfortable silence. Jack felt satisfied with the events of the morning; the only dark spot was that one moment when she shied away from him, but he tried to focus on the good parts. Anyway, he was sure she would come around if they spent more time together.

If only he could ride out with her like this every day…

"Will you help me stay in practice while you're in town?" he asked, hoping he didn't sound as desperate as he felt. "I could use a teammate to keep me sharp."

Amy rotated her shoulder and grimaced. "I don't think I'll be much help for the next few days as I recover from the workout today, but I'd like that."

Jack smiled. "Great. Come over tomorrow morning and we can walk through the moves. I promise I won't make you throw anything."

Amy agreed, and then Jack walked her out to the truck she'd used to get to his house. After their hands and eyes lingered for a few extra seconds, he forced himself to let go and watch as she climbed into the vehicle and went on her way.

He knew she needed to leave, had family obliga-
tions, but damn, he didn't want her to go. As the truck
disappeared around the corner, he could only console
himself with the knowledge that he would see her again
the next morning.

In the meantime, he had some matters to discuss
with his family, and there was no time like the present.

Chapter Six

Jack walked back to the house, wondering if it was even possible to make everyone in the family happy. He would just need to try, he supposed.

Since nobody was in the kitchen or living room, Jack went in search of his mother in the place he knew he was most likely to find her: a guest-room-turned-sanctuary that she occasionally called her woman-cave. With bright sunlight streaming through the windows and light, happy colors everywhere, calling it a cave seemed a bit of a misnomer.

Jack's mother was sitting by the window in her favorite chair, reading. She looked so comfortable, so content, that Jack almost decided to forget the whole thing and not break the older woman's sense of peace. But then he thought of Tom's worry and knocked lightly on the open door.

"Mom, you got a minute?"

His mother chuckled as she closed her book. "For a person who used to be so busy, I seem to have all the time in the world since I officially became an old lady and my boys started taking care of things for me."

Jack didn't think they'd "taken care of things" particularly well, but only said, "I'm going to find Tom. I actually need to talk to both of you."

Jack's mom looked curious, but not worried. "He's out in the barn, most likely. I'll go fix up a few sandwiches and we can eat while you say whatever's on your mind."

Jack nodded and left for the barn. After a little searching he found his brother cleaning a horse's hooves, a frown of concentration on his face. Although, Jack corrected himself, it seemed like Tom wore that frown nearly all the time these days. Jack should have done something about this months ago.

Jack wondered if Tom ever told the horses his problems when he was in the barn alone, but he immediately dismissed the idea. Tom would never confide in a horse, which was one of the clearest indicators, Jack thought, that he shouldn't be running a ranch. Tom did what needed to be done, but he just wasn't a cowboy at heart. Though what else he wanted to do was anybody's guess.

Jack pulled himself out of his own head when Tom glanced up at him. "Why are you watching me like that?" he asked.

"Nothing," Jack said. "Just letting my mind wander. Mom's making us some lunch."

Tom nodded and quickly finished his task before joining Jack on the walk to the house. "Did you have a good time with Amy today?" he asked.

Jack nodded but didn't elaborate. Now was not the time to get lost on the subject of Amy.

In the kitchen, their mother was just setting three plates on the table, and the two men took their seats. "So, what did you want to discuss with us, Jack?"

Tom gave Jack a surprised look, but Jack ignored it and spoke more honestly to her than he or Tom had in a long time. "Mom, we haven't wanted to say anything because we knew it would worry you, but the ranch is losing money. Badly. And Tom's been doing the best he can, but he shouldn't be carrying this burden all on his own when he doesn't even want to be here."

The older woman looked back and forth between her sons and Tom glared at Jack. Jack shrugged. "Sorry, but it's true, and Mom deserves to know. And you deserve to do something besides worry about bills constantly."

Their mother's eyes settled on Tom. "Are things truly that bad?"

Tom's glare turned to a look of apology as he turned toward his mom. "I just didn't have the heart to tell you I was running this place into the ground," he said quietly.

After a beat of silence, the older woman shook her head. "What is the matter with you two? I thought I raised you better than to hide something like this from me. Tom, you go get any paperwork you have right this instant and we're going to sort this all out right now."

It was Jack's turn to be surprised. He hadn't heard his mother speak to them like that since they were children. Tom slunk out of his chair and down the hall to the office. Soon he was back with a stack of paperwork and they ate their sandwiches as the true state of the ranch became clear to all three of them.

It was even worse than Jack had guessed. Once they'd gone through every scrap of paper, their mom leaned back and pushed her reading glasses to the top of her head. "Well, it seems we don't have many options, boys," she said finally. "We can keep losing money until we go bankrupt, or we sell the ranch and move on while we're still able. Tom, I know you've never wanted to live here—do you have someplace to go if we sell?"

Tom flushed. "There's a girl I met online a while back who I'd like to meet. She lives in Boston. I'd like to spend some time out that way, get a job and see where things go with her."

Their mother nodded as if this was the most normal thing in the world, though Jack was still having trouble absorbing it all. Tom wanted to move to Boston to be with a girl he'd met on the internet? Before he could reconcile all this with what he knew about his brother, their mom turned to him. "With my part of the sale I'm sure I'll be able to find a place in town that I can afford. So that just leaves you, Jack. I know you always wanted to buy out your brother's stake in this place and keep the ranch running, but I just don't see a way for us to hold out that long."

It broke Jack's heart to think of his future rodeo school being sold to some stranger while he went off to…do something. He could keep roping for a few more years, maybe, but after that? He'd never considered doing anything but come back here to Spring Valley for good.

Still, his mother was willing to give up her home without a complaint, and Tom had put his own life on hold for God only knew how long. He couldn't exactly ask them to fight to keep the ranch and risk bankruptcy just so he could keep his dream alive.

Jack nodded. "I'll land on my feet, whatever happens," he assured her.

The old woman stood. "It's settled then. We'll put the ranch up for sale. It's the only way," she said, looking at Jack as she said it.

She knew exactly how difficult this was for him, Jack was sure. He was also sure she was hurting at the thought of leaving her home, even though she didn't show a hint of her feelings. Jack gave her a small smile and nodded in agreement.

"I'll stay to help get everything settled," Tom said, his voice so somber that Jack knew he was feeling the loss, too.

Their mother agreed instantly, her hand hitting the table lightly, like she was a judge banging her gavel. "Then it's settled. Is there anything else you wanted to discuss with us, Jack?"

Jack shook his head and she stood up. He hadn't said anything for a long while, but he still kept his mouth shut. What was there for him to say, really?

His mom gave him one last curious look. "I tell you, I wasn't expecting *this* to be our topic of conversation at all," she said, waving her hand to indicate the house.

Jack finally felt his tongue unstuck from the roof

of his mouth. "What did you think I wanted to talk to you about?" he asked.

"Oh, nothing," his mother said in a tone that meant obviously something. "Perhaps something regarding you and Ms. McNeal. But it may be a bit early for that, I suppose."

Before Jack could say a thing, his mother was on her way out of the room. "I'll get started on a list of Realtors," she said as she disappeared back into her woman-cave.

Tom gave Jack a quick grin before leaving the table himself. "I'm going to work out in the barn for a while," he said with a spring in his step.

Jack just sat there at the table, his brain trying to absorb what had happened, what he'd instigated. He tried to tell himself it was all for the best, but it was hard to believe.

AMY SAT INSIDE the truck, though she had parked in front of the McNeal house minutes ago, a nervous fluttering in her stomach. She knew she should get inside, that she was already late, but her mind was a flurry of activity and refused to settle down. What if they asked her about Jack once she got in there? She wasn't sure what to tell them. Heck, she wasn't even sure what to tell herself.

Everything had been going so well, and then Jack had pushed back a hair from her face and she'd panicked, and it frustrated her to no end that it was all because of Armand. He'd acted just that same sweet way when they first met, and it made her want to run from

Jack as fast as she could. But she knew that was un-fair. He *was* sweet and kind, and she knew it. So why couldn't her heart accept that and move on?

Amy sighed and leaned back. If only things could be simple, the way they had been when she was seventeen and in love with the nice cowboy. She still felt strong feelings toward him, along with a desire so strong it surprised her every time she laid eyes on him, but her head was so full of worry and doubts that she didn't know how to relax and accept any intimacy.

If her siblings asked, she would just say they were rebuilding a friendship. It wasn't exactly a lie, even if it didn't tell the whole story. Since she didn't even know what the whole story was, it would have to do.

As she unbuckled her seat belt, another concern oc-curred to her: Should she tell them about her scheduled meeting with her half sister? Would they be excited, or maybe a little hurt that she felt the need to find more family, like they weren't enough?

She stepped out of the truck, considering what to do on that account, and didn't even notice Jose barrel-ing out the front door until he picked her up in a bone-cracking hug that made her give a loud, startled laugh.

"Big sis!" he said once he set her down and wrapped an arm around her shoulder. "There you are! Ma was about to have us send the dogs out to search for you."

Amy chuckled at the idea of Buster, Pop's old shep-herd, searching any farther than his dog bed. Jose, Di-ego's twin, could be frustrating at times, but he was also the guy you wanted around if you needed to forget your worries. He led her into the house shouting, "Don't worry, Ma! I found her!"

Diego glanced up from his spot on the couch. "Where did he find you?" he asked.

Amy rolled her eyes. "In the driveway, climbing out of your truck. Thanks, by the way," she said, tossing him his keys.

He caught them with a nod. Amy waited for Jose to ask where she'd been, with whom, and what scandalous acts she'd done there as he mined for his next joke, but he said nothing. Amy guessed she had Diego to thank for that. He was the only person who could even attempt to keep Jose in line.

Soon Brock, Cassie, Jose, Diego and Amy were all sitting in the living room together, where they had been relegated when they, as Ma put it, "kept getting in her hair while she was trying to make a decent meal for all of them."

"Carter and Zach didn't get kicked out," Jose grumbled. "It's clear who Ma's favorite twins are."

Brock shrugged. "They're way cuter than you two."

Jose put on an offended air. "Excuse me, we're *adorable*."

"And they follow directions better," Brock added.

Jose grinned and nodded. "Well, that's true enough."

Amy listened to her brothers' banter, but a good deal of her attention was on her right arm. Now that she was relaxed, it was clear she'd pushed her muscles way too far, and her bicep ached like crazy. She kneaded it gingerly.

"Is there a problem with your arm?" Cassie asked, watching with her sharp doctor's eyes.

Amy stopped her ministrations. "It's fine. Just a little sore from exercising this morning."

Jose snorted in what was clearly an exaggerated attempt to start a joke, but Diego stepped on his foot and Jose's snort turned into an innocent cough. Amy gave Diego a quick glance of thanks, and he sent her a little smile. She didn't need Jose to start commenting on what "exercise" she could have been up to.

The moment passed and Diego turned to Jose. "Now that we're all together, will you tell us about your new secret girlfriend? He's been waiting all week to talk about her," Diego explained to the gathered siblings.

Jose held up his hand, and Amy could see he was enjoying building the anticipation. "I will talk about her when we are *all* together, including Ma and Pop."

"If Zach and Carter are in the room, you better keep it G-rated, little brother," Brock pointed out.

Jose gave Brock his widest, most innocent smile. "Come on, Broccoli, you know my stories are fun for all ages."

"What about the story about the night you spent in Atlantic City? That was definitely adults-only," Amy threw in, happy to be joking with her brothers.

Jose's smile became much less innocent. "Oh yeah, that was a crazy night. Cassie, you haven't heard this. So, I was in Atlantic City for the weekend…" Jose started, launching into his story.

Amy leaned back and looked at her brothers and soon-to-be sister. She hadn't realized how much she'd missed this part of being a family. Just sitting around, talking about nothing. She'd been home so rarely, and had always had Jack's cloud hanging over her, that it seemed ages since she and her brothers had talked like this.

"Time to set the table!" Ma called from the kitchen.

At the same time, two little whirlwinds rushed into the room balancing plates and silverware. Amy watched her young nephews hand out jobs, as directed by their grandmother. Cassie seemed grateful that Jose's story was left unfinished as she followed her children into the dining room.

"What are we having?" Amy asked the crowd as she sniffed the air.

"Sweet potatoes and okra and pork something. I forget. It's really yummy!" Carter told her all in a rush.

Jose gave the young twin a shake of his head. "You got to taste the food? I got kicked out just for suggesting I try a little. That's not fair!" he called into the kitchen.

Ma walked in with a plate piled high with pork chops. "You're not competing with a pair of four-year-olds, Jose," she said before giving Zach and Carter a big grin. "Let's go get you two some soda pop," she added, hustling them back into the kitchen.

Jose crossed his arms. "*We* never got soda pop when we were kids. It was always 'that stuff will rot your teeth.'"

Brock set the plates at each place while the rest of them took the other tasks. "She's taking her job as a grandmother very seriously. Soda pop, desserts, she even started up the candy bird thing."

Amy looked up, surprised. She could remember every trip to her grandparents including a visit from the "candy bird," a magical creature who left candy for young children.

"Ma said she would *never ever* do the candy bird. Remember how much she grumbled on the drive home while we ate our Tootsie Pops?" Diego said, sounding as astonished as Amy felt.

"Oh, I know," Brock said, "That didn't stop the candy bird from making an appearance a couple weeks ago."

Ma, Pop and the twins chose this moment to make their appearance in the dining room with the last of the food, the two young boys each carrying a cup of cola. As they sat down, Jose pointed a finger at his adopted mother. "So, the candy bird comes here now?" he asked, sounding a little more indignant than a grown man should about candy.

Zach and Carter immediately launched into the story of the candy bird. "If we're really good and leave the window open, Nana Sarah says the candy bird will come again soon!" Carter finished excitedly.

Ma blushed. "Pop reminded me about the candy bird, and I thought it might be nice to—er…send her our address," she said, looking around significantly, daring any of her children to ruin this for her grandsons.

"Come on, guys, everyone loves the candy bird," Amy said as she piled food onto her plate. "Just look at the boys," she finished, pointing to the sparkly-eyed children.

The first bite of food overshadowed the gentle bickering, and Amy's heart felt full at that moment. Really, there was nothing like home and family. Even when they were all adults, things didn't change, and for that she was grateful. As much as she enjoyed her lifestyle, it forced her to be a grown-up all the time. Here, she could have an argument about the rightful existence of a fictional bird that brought children sweets.

"Fine!" Ma said, sounding exasperated. "I'll let the candy bird know you'd like her to bring enough treats for the rest of you lot, too. Ya happy?"

Jose settled back and speared a bite of pork chop with his fork. "Extremely," he said, looking very satisfied with himself.

The family settled down and ate quietly for a short while before Diego spoke up. "Now that we've cleared up important topics like the candy bird, we can move on to Jose's new girlfriend he's been dying to tell us about."

Jose looked up, all innocence. "Brother, I have been protecting my amour's privacy, not withholding information. It's actually quite gentlemanly of me."

Diego gave Jose a look and Jose dropped the act. "Okay, her name's Kate and I met her at one of the ranches outside Dallas when I was looking at livestock out there. She's a riding school instructor."

Amy wasn't sure why Jose had built up this whole thing to tell them about a girl he'd met. She'd assumed the woman would be someone they knew or famous or something. Everyone else seemed to be confused, too.

"Well, she sounds nice. When will we meet her?" Ma asked.

"In a week," Jose said, looking straight at Pop. "She's going to interview to take over the riding school for you."

Amy let out a long, low breath. There it was.

They had all been concerned about Pop and the toll that running the riding school and ranch was taking on him at his age, but telling him that hadn't ended well in the past.

Pop slowly put down his fork and looked up at his adopted son. "What was that, Jose?"

Jose looked serious for one of the few times in his life. "In a week Kate's coming here to interview so she can take over the day-to-day riding school operations. She can live here and stay in Brock's old room, since he doesn't need it anymore. I'll pay her from my own pocket if I need to. And if you don't think you need help," he said pointedly, "the riding school and the kids are the ones who will suffer."

Pop and Jose stared at each other, and the rest of the family watched, quiet. "You've thought this whole thing out, haven't you?" Pop asked.

Jose nodded.

There was another second of silence before Pop nodded back. "Fine, I'll meet with her. But I'm not promising anything," he added.

The tension in the air seemed to dissolve and Jose

went back to his usual smiling self. "I knew I was your favorite," he said.

Exclamations of protest broke out around the table, and the rest of dinner was spent arguing over which of the children was, in fact, the favorite.

After Brock, Cassie and the boys left that evening, Jose stood up and stretched. "I don't know about you two, but I woke up too early this morning. I'm heading to bed. And," he added, pointing to his twin, "I'm taking Brock's room tonight. No more bunk beds for me."

After he left, Diego commented, "I didn't know we could call Brock's room now that he lives next door."

Amy shrugged. "Jose beat you to it, fair and square."

Diego nodded in his usual good-natured way. "How was today at Jack's?" he asked.

Though Amy had been relieved she didn't need to discuss her activities with the whole family, the events of the day hadn't been far from her thoughts the entire evening. She looked down at the couch and picked at one of the faded roses on the upholstery. "We did some roping."

She didn't know how to express what it felt like to be so in sync with someone, or how much she wished she could just fall into his arms without thinking about Morocco and everything that had happened there.

Diego seemed to sense some of that, though. "You don't need to make any decisions right now. Just do what you enjoy and what makes you happy, okay?"

Amy nodded and Jose stood. "I'm heading to bed myself. See you in the morning."

Amy said good-night and slipped onto the bench

that ran beneath the large front window of the house. She thought about all the times she'd sat there, praying Jack wouldn't appear and want to talk to her. Now all she wanted was to see him and hear his voice.

Amy glanced at her phone, briefly considering calling him before putting it away. It was late, and besides, she'd see him the next day. That should be soon enough to satisfy her.

But it wasn't.

She wanted to give herself over to her feelings like they'd done in the barn. Shut her mind off and allow her heart to accept who he was without her baggage from the past few weeks tainting the moment.

Just as she decided to call him despite the time, headlights flashed across her face as a truck pulled into the driveway, then went dark as it parked. She would know that truck anywhere, even in the pitch dark, and Amy hopped up and ran outside to see what Jack was doing in front of her house so late in the evening.

JACK PUT THE truck in Park and killed the headlights, his heart jumping at the sight of Amy in the big window, her form outlined by the light behind her. He had been driving just to think, and had ended up at her house without even realizing where he was headed. He'd gone into the driveway so he could turn around—or at least that was what he told himself—when he saw Amy in the window, as if she was waiting for him.

He opened up the truck door as she ran down the porch steps, and without thinking about it, he wrapped her in a tight hug and pressed his lips to hers. She seemed just as desperate for the intimacy, and it was a long moment before they parted. Any hesitancy Amy had shown that morning was long gone, if her tight hold on him was any indication.

Once they could breathe again, Amy gave a little sigh. "I was just thinking about you," she told him, leaning her head against his shoulder.

He didn't respond, just held her close. He didn't know what had changed in the few hours since he'd last seen her, but he wasn't about to do anything that might ruin it. She wanted to be in his arms, and she'd been thinking about him. A thrill of love shot through his veins. If he was honest, he was *always* thinking about her, but he kept that thought to himself.

"What are you doing here?" she asked.

"I went out for a drive to clear my thoughts," Jack explained.

She lifted her head to look him in the eye. "What's the trouble?"

Jack tried to give her a reassuring smile, but he wasn't sure how well he succeeded. "I talked to Tom and my mother, and we've decided we don't have any choice but to sell the ranch."

Amy's eyes widened at the news, and Jack knew she understood how hard this was for him. His childhood home owned by some strangers, his rodeo school dream up in smoke.

He shrugged, trying to seem lighthearted about the whole thing. "We just don't have the funds to keep it going, and it's not likely I'll ever win big enough in competitions to get the money I'd need to renovate the place anyway, so really, this is for the best. I'll land on my feet."

Jack knew by her expression that she saw right through his words, so he stopped talking and just hugged her close, gathering strength from her.

"Are you going to be leaving Spring Valley for good after that?" she asked, and he thought her voice caught in her throat for a second.

"I'm so sorry," she said in a whisper. "If I hadn't meddled—"

"Then we would have lost even more money and would end up with the same outcome, only worse," he told her.

He saw that in her eyes she still felt guilt over her part in this decision, and he lifted her chin until she was looking him in the eye. "This is what needs to happen, Amy. You didn't create our mess, and you shouldn't feel bad for pointing out that we were hiding from it. Thank you for stopping us from keeping our heads in the sand until we went bankrupt."

Then he leaned down and kissed her, and neither of them said anything for a long time.

"Any idea when all this will happen?" Amy asked eventually, her forehead pressed against his.

"It'll be at least a month," he answered, "and probably longer if the ranch sits on the market a bit."

Finally, after another long silence, they broke apart. "I better get home," Jack said. "But I'll see you tomorrow, right?"

Amy gave him a smile that looked slightly forced. "I'll be there," she said.

Then, with a little wave, she turned toward her house and he climbed into his truck. Jack waited until she was inside and the light in the living room was turned off, then started the truck's engine.

In a month, Amy would leave once again for her adventures. In a month, maybe a little more, the ranch he'd always thought of as home would be gone.

When the time came, there would be some very difficult decisions to make. But until then, he was going to enjoy this month for all it was worth.

Chapter Seven

Amy awoke the next morning feeling light-headed. For the second night in a row, she'd gotten very little sleep and it was starting to take its toll on her. She rolled out of bed, had a quick breakfast with her parents, Diego and Jose, and then asked to borrow Diego's keys.

"What, you aren't going to stick around here and have quality time with your brothers?" Jose demanded.

"I'm helping Jack practice roping to stay in shape until he finds a new partner," she told him.

Jose seemed about to say something, but Diego put a hand on his twin's shoulder and Jose quieted down. Amy thought, not for the first time, that Jose really shouldn't be allowed out in the world without Diego nearby to balance him out. "You never let me have any fun, you know," she heard Jose whisper to Diego, who took no notice of his brother.

"I'll be back in a few hours, and we can do quality time then," Amy said, ignoring their interaction. Jose shook his head dramatically. "Too little too late, sister. And I was going to tell you where Ma hides the soda pop."

Diego rolled his eyes. "It's in the fridge. Have a good time, Ames."

Amy waved goodbye to him over her shoulder as she walked out.

Her morning at the Stuarts was much the same as before, except for two things: one, she could hardly lift her right arm to shoulder height and had to practice without an actual rope in her hand, and two, the mood of each person in the Stuart household had changed, though they all seemed to be taking pains to hide it. Tom was certainly happier, more relaxed, and Jack couldn't completely conceal how at a loss he felt.

Amy's heart ached for Jack. He'd always held tightly to his dream, had been so sure as a young man that he would be able to reach his goals. Now he was faced with giving them up completely, and Amy could tell it hurt him badly.

Amy also had a selfish reason for not wanting Stuart Ranch to sell. If Jack left Spring Valley for good, would that destroy even the tiny chance that they might be able to make something work between them? As it was, his time on the rodeo circuit and her travels, let alone the baggage and other difficulties that lay between them, made a relationship seemed laughably impossible. Take away Spring Valley, the one connection they really had, and it seemed there was no hope at all.

She tried hard not to think about it, but it was clear she and Jack were both preoccupied, and she almost felt relief when they finally called an end to the practice session.

As Amy and Jack brushed down the horses, Jack

brought up a topic she hadn't even thought of since his news the previous night. "So, have you thought about how you're going to get to Austin on Wednesday?"

It took Amy a moment to remember why she was going to Austin, and then a burst of some combination of emotions too complex to name flowed through her. She was going to be meeting her half sister in just a few days. "I—I guess I'll just borrow Pop's truck for the day," she said, not really liking the answer.

If she borrowed the truck, she'd feel obligated to explain why, and Amy just didn't know if she was ready to talk about it with her adopted family yet.

"How about I drive you instead?" Jack asked.

Amy looked up at him in surprise, but before she could protest, he added, "I should go in anyway to get the property listed with some Realtors. And you never know, you might need someone around."

She was still about to insist she could handle it on her own when he looked into her eyes and made her arguments for her. "I know you've thought a lot about this, and I know you can take care of yourself whatever happens, but you shouldn't have to."

Amy closed her mouth, took a moment to let this thought settle in her mind. She was so used to relying on only herself in every situation that it seemed odd to need someone else, but it also gave her a sense of comfort. Finally, she agreed. "That would be nice. Thanks."

She grasped his hand and felt the familiar rush of electricity through her veins. She couldn't know where this would go, but she knew that for the moment she was happy.

When Amy arrived home a short while later, Jose and Diego were sitting in the living room arguing over something. They stopped when she arrived, but she could feel the tension between them. "What's going on?" she asked as she sunk into the old couch.

Jose rolled his eyes. "Diego has no vision and wants to keep us living at the poverty line instead of believing in me," he said.

Amy looked over to Diego, who seemed just as irritated, though without the sarcastic edge Jose employed. "Our business is just getting off the ground, and I'm sorry if I don't think now's the time to start putting what little money we've made into other ventures, even if some guy you know told you it was a 'sure thing,'" Diego retorted.

Amy felt a sort of guilty happiness that the twins were so caught up in their own lives that they would hopefully avoid asking about her own. Between her lunch with her half sister, guilt about Jack losing his ranch, and the confusing nature of her relationship with Jack, everything felt like a land mine she wasn't prepared to discuss. Better to talk about the two of them and their issues rather than hers. And maybe she could even help them somehow.

"What is this 'sure thing'?" she asked Jose.

"It shouldn't really matter," he answered, "at least not to a brother who's supposed to trust me."

With that, Jose stood and walked out of the room. Diego sighed and dropped back against the couch. "Sometimes he can be such a pain in the ass," he told Amy.

Amy shrugged. "Yeah, but I don't think that'll be changing anytime soon."

Diego nodded. "And, as usual, he's going to get his way. He knows I'll let him take the money if he pushes hard enough."

Amy agreed. They all knew Diego and Jose well enough by now to know how they worked. "How's your rodeo stock business going?" she asked, trying to understand the situation a little better.

He sighed again, making it clear that it wasn't exactly pleasant territory, either. "We're making enough to survive," he said.

That sounded like a big red flag to Amy. "Are you enjoying it?"

Diego didn't answer. Before Amy could ask another question, Jose was back with a cup of soda, his grin settled into its normal position on his face. "Sorry about that," he told both of his siblings. "This is something we can figure out later, Diego. I'm only here through tonight, and I don't want to spend it arguing when I can pry into my sister's life instead."

Before Amy could process what he'd said, Jose set his glass down on the coffee table, flopped onto the couch and put an arm around her. "So, Ames, how are things with you and Jack? Starting up the old flame? Is it love?"

Amy wasn't sure if Jose was teasing her, genuinely curious, or just trying to irritate Diego, but now she was stuck, and she knew Jose would refuse to take "no comment" as an answer. She shuddered to think of the mayhem Jose might cause if she didn't satisfy his curiosity at least a little bit.

"Jack and I," she began, choosing her words with care, "are trying to find out who we are after all these years."

Jose looked unimpressed. "That's it? No declarations of love and lifelong happiness? At least tell me one of you has proposed a secret elopement in one of those weird foreign countries you love so much."

An image of her and Jack walking along a beach, her long white wedding dress trailing in the sand, made her heart jump before she quashed the thought.

If she let herself dream like that and it didn't come true, Amy wasn't sure she'd ever be able to recover. After all, she knew better than anyone that a good start to a relationship didn't mean things would end well at all. It was just best not to dream at all.

"Nope," Amy said, to both herself and Jose. "We're just dating. Kind of. *Casually*," she emphasized, even though she knew there was nothing casual about the way Jack looked at her.

Or about the way she looked at Jack, for that matter.

Amy wanted desperately to change the topic, but the only other thing in her mind was meeting her half sister, and—

And why couldn't she talk about that with Jose and Diego, her brothers *who were also adopted*?

They always felt like such close siblings to her, she often forgot they were adopted, too, despite their differences. Brock was technically adopted as well, but Ma and Pop were his biological aunt and uncle. He'd lived with his real parents until they died when he was eight. If anyone in the family would understand her situation, it would be the twins.

Suddenly, she was bursting to talk to them about what only minutes before she'd been carefully keeping to herself. She took a deep breath and went for it. "Hey, have you guys ever thought about your family?"

"If you're accusing us of not coming home enough," Jose answered, crossing his arms, "that's a lot of talk from a woman who only comes home—"

"No, Jose," Amy said, cutting him off. "Your *family*. Your biological family."

"Oh, that," Jose said, settling back into the couch and putting his feet up. "Nope. Who needs 'em?"

Amy felt a rush of disappointment. Was she the only one who was curious about her real parents, her other siblings?

"Jose," Diego said, his voice quietly disapproving, "This is Amy. We can tell her."

Jose waved a hand in the air, as if to say Diego could do whatever he liked, but he wasn't going to participate. Amy turned to Diego and waited.

"When we turned eighteen," he told her, his voice hushed, as if he was afraid someone was going to overhear, "we dug into our adoption papers and found our parents' names. We found them and tried to contact them."

Amy was nearly breathless, waiting to hear what they'd found. And amazed she didn't know about this. Where had she been?

But she knew the answer to that. She'd been away

at college, hiding from Jack and dealing with the loss of her picture-perfect future. So focused on herself that she hadn't been around as her brothers grappled with growing up and finding out who they were, where they were from.

"Anyway, it didn't go well," Diego finished quickly, leaning back on the couch himself to show his story was complete.

Amy waited another few seconds, sure he wouldn't just leave it at that. "That's all you're going to tell me?" she asked.

"What else is there to say?" Jose countered, standing up. "They didn't want us when we were born and they didn't want us as adults, except maybe as a way to get money, somehow." With that, he stalked out of the room for the second time in ten minutes.

Amy watched him go, not sure what to say. "He was the one who really wanted to find them," Diego explained to her once Jose was gone. "It hit him hard that they weren't interested in us."

Amy's heart broke for her little brother who always seemed so happy and carefree. Diego had warned her that he had difficulties of his own, but this was her first real glimpse at one. What other burdens was he carrying under that smile?

"Why did you want to know?" Diego asked, taking her attention from the empty doorway. "Have you been doing some searching of your own?"

"A woman from California emailed me," she confessed. "She's my half sister, apparently. I'm meeting her Wednesday for lunch."

Diego nodded encouragingly. "That sounds like a better start than we had. I'm sure it'll go well, and we're here for you if you need us, you know."

Amy hugged her brother tight. Then he stood. "I better go find Jose and tell him he can have the money for his 'sure thing' scheme. That'll put him in a better mood."

Before he made it to the door, though, Amy had one more question for him: "Did you talk to Ma and Pop about looking for your parents?"

Diego shook his head. "I think they would've been supportive, but we didn't want to do that to them, you know?"

Amy nodded. She knew. Diego walked out of the room, leaving her alone with her thoughts.

Amy spent the rest of the evening, and the better part of the following day, only able to half focus on the people and places around her. The only time she was able to truly be in the moment were the few hours she spent on a horse roping with Jack.

Now that her meeting with her half sister felt real and was looming so near, it engulfed her. What if she had more family out there, a whole tribe of people she'd never met? What if she came away from all this as disappointed as Jose was? Or what if she found another family who was loving, who wanted her to be a part of their lives?

And she also had so many questions about Maryanne and the information she held. How were they similar, and what traits did Amy have that she got from her mother, their common parent? Did Maryanne know their mother, or was she adopted, too?

Amy suddenly wished she'd spent more time emailing this woman before agreeing to meet. She was going into this with so many questions.

Wednesday morning, as she buckled herself into Jack's truck, Amy had a quick moment of panic and started to think it might be best if she called the whole thing off. Before she could say anything to that effect, though, Jack leaned over and put his hand on her shoulder. "It's going to all be fine, I know it," he said, his voice quiet and soothing.

She looked at him and her heart calmed a little. So long as he was nearby, it would be.

JACK DROVE THE two hours to Austin keeping up a continual stream of conversation, trying to keep Amy's nerves from getting the better of her. As relaxed as he sounded, he had his own knot of anxiety in his stomach. He could hardly imagine what a big deal this was for her, and his sympathy made him feel itchy with the need to make it better. But for the moment, there was nothing he could do but be there in the truck with her.

At last, they entered the city, and Jack thought with relief that it would all be over soon, for better or worse. He heard Amy's phone ding and watched her out of the corner of his eye. She stared at her phone for a long while, and it didn't take long for him to see that something was wrong. Jack pulled into a parking lot, cut the engine, and turned to Amy.

"She can't make our lunch," Amy said, still not

taking her eyes from her phone. "Work stuff came up at the conference and she won't be able to get away. And she's leaving for California this afternoon, so we can't reschedule."

Amy looked up then, and the disappointment in her eyes cut him to the quick. "She says she's really, really sorry," Amy finished quietly.

Jack unbuckled his seat belt and pulled Amy tight against him. "She *should* be sorry," he said, angry on her behalf.

After a minute of silence, Amy pulled away and sat back in her seat. She wasn't crying, but she still seemed upset. "Things happen, I guess. I hope you don't mind me hanging around while you meet with Realtors," she said.

Jack shook his head as he started the truck's engine. "No, we're heading back to Spring Valley. I can do all that online."

For a second, he thought she would argue, or maybe if he was lucky she would say something sarcastic. Instead she just agreed, lay back against the headrest and closed her eyes.

The ride home was quiet, and even when Jack asked Amy if she'd like to stop for lunch, she did no more than shake her head.

As they got close to Spring Valley, Amy became more animated. "I'm feeling much better. Sorry about that back there. I was just startled and needed a little while to process the change. But really, I'm fine now."

Jack wasn't sure he believed her, but he nodded. "How about I take you home for a little while, and then we go out to dinner? I could use another lava cake, and I sure would like to see that blue dress again. Or something else. Or nothing at all, if you like," he said, hoping for a laugh or an eye roll.

Amy pinched her lips together, the only hint he got that she was at all amused. "Lava cake sounds good," she said, but she didn't sound very excited.

When they were parked in front of the McNeal house once again, Jack turned to her. "Would you like me to come inside with you?"

Amy gave him a small smile and shook her head. "I'm going to take a nap. I haven't been sleeping well, and I think a little rest is the thing I need most right now."

Jack watched her walk into the house, but didn't start his truck. He could see how disappointed she was, and he knew he needed to do something to help. He was pretty sure there was a way. There was the chance, of course, that it would blow up in his face and make her absolutely furious.

But he'd take that risk if it might give her some comfort.

AMY AWOKE SLOWLY, feeling a little groggy but better. She was surprised how the loss of the chance to meet her biological sibling hit her so hard, and she told herself for the fiftieth time or so that she had plenty of family, and she could always keep emailing Mary-anne to get answers to her questions. It didn't make the cloud hanging over her dissipate entirely, but she knew it would in time.

It took Amy several seconds to realize she was hearing voices downstairs, and that one of those voices was Jack's.

What's Jack doing here? she wondered. Was it already time for their date?

A quick glance at her phone confirmed it was still too early for that, so she got out of bed and went to investigate. Jack was sitting with Ma and Pop at the dining table, drinking coffee. When she walked in, they all looked up at her. She waited for them to explain what was going on, even though she was pretty sure she could guess based on the slightly guilty look on Jack's face.

It didn't take long. Ma and Pop both stood and engulfed her in a big hug. "We're so sorry about what happened today, sweetie," Ma said as she squeezed Amy so hard she could barely breathe.

Amy looked at Jack for confirmation that he'd told them. He gave her an apologetic shrug, but before she could process his decision to tell her parents without her permission, Pop spoke. "We think you should go to California next weekend and meet your sister. Get your questions answered. We'll help any way we can."

Ma nodded. "And I think I should go with you. For moral support and all. Or to break down her door if need be."

Amy hugged her family tight and, after a minute, threw Jack a look she hoped he'd be able to interpret. It was gratitude. She knew he was trying so hard to give her what she needed, even if it meant she left for days when they already had so little time together.

Fewer than four weeks.

Jack stood, tipped his hat at her and mouthed *be back at seven* before taking his leave.

Amy allowed herself to be shuttled into a chair and given coffee while Ma and Pop discussed precisely what would need to happen in order for this California trip to be a success.

"The first thing that we should do is email this Maryanne to let her know we'll be there in ten days—you will, won't you dear?"

It took a second for Amy to realize a response was required of her, and she thought for a moment. Was this what she wanted?

The devastation from a few hours ago made the answer clear. She *had* to know. "I'll email her right now," Amy said decisively.

The excitement that had disappeared in such a flash a few hours before began building again. And it was all because of Jack.

After a couple hours of planning and an enthusiastic response from Maryanne to Amy's carefully worded email, Amy dressed for dinner and was at the door when Jack arrived, running down to him before he even had a chance to park.

As she climbed into the truck, he glanced at her sheepishly. "Sure you still want to go out with me?"

In response, Amy leaned over and gave him a big kiss full on his mouth. Then she smiled. "Thank you. Because of you, I'll be meeting my sister after all. What made you decide to talk to them?"

Jack looked relieved. "I was half sure you'd hate

me for telling your parents about it, but I thought they could help you in ways I couldn't. And I was hoping you'd decide that they deserved to know and would forgive me eventually," he said.

Amy grimaced a little as she heard her own advice being used on her. "I should have told them days ago. I'm just embarrassed I needed you to do it for me. And while I'm not sure I like being saved, it's rather nice to have a knight in shining armor ready to rescue me."

"I don't think you've ever needed someone to rescue you. I was just trying to help in the only way I could," he told her.

Amy felt the tears prick in her eyes. How could he make her feel so loved and cared for in just a few sentences? Best of all, she knew he was being honest, that she could trust him. For the first time in weeks, when Armand's face popped into her head, she was able to shake him off as easily as a horse's tail shooing a fly. He had no place in this thing with her and Jack.

Jack cranked the engine, leaning back after it began to purr. "Should we go get some dinner?" he asked.

Amy agreed and settled back into the passenger seat, letting her feelings for this good, kind man wash over her.

ON SATURDAY MORNING, Jack woke early, his mind immediately on Amy. Something had changed between them since their drive to Austin on Wednesday, and it filled Jack with hope. He didn't know exactly what it was, but all of Amy's little hesitancies and moments of worry seemed gone. The way she held his hand as they sat together at dinner that night, along with her tiny acts of affection during their roping sessions over the past couple days, made him think that maybe they could make this thing work. And by God, he wanted it to work.

They had spent so many hours laughing and flirting that for the first time, Jack wondered if Amy would be willing to change her life a bit in order to keep him in it. He wasn't ready to ask her yet—they still had time, after all—but he couldn't help but imagine that it was possible.

Jack pulled himself out of those memories and instead thought of the day ahead. He and Tom would spend the next several hours sprucing up the ranch a bit in order to help it sell, and then he was going to Amy's in the evening.

As he finished dressing and settled his cowboy hat on his head, Jack's phone started to ring. He looked at the number but didn't recognize it and couldn't think who would be calling him at such an early hour. He swiped his phone, wondering who it could be.

"Hello?" he prompted, putting the phone to his ear.

"Is this Jack Stuart?" said a voice he only vaguely recognized.

As soon as he answered in the affirmative, the mystery man exclaimed, "Jack! Sorry to call you so early, but this is important. You haven't gotten a new roping partner yet, have you?"

Jack's eyes widened as he realized where he'd heard that voice before. He'd gone to the NFR in Las Vegas as merely a spectator the year before and had met the second-place roping team. "Is this Sam Evans?" he asked, incredulous.

A chuckle came through from the other end of the call. "I was hoping you'd remember me. So, do you still need a teammate?"

Sam's words slowly worked their way into Jack's brain. "I sure do," he answered, trying not to let his excitement run away with him.

"Great! I need someone, and I think you and I could be great together. How about you come out here to Cheyenne next weekend? Unless you want to hold out for a better offer, of course," he said, sounding almost amused at the idea of a better offer.

"No!" Jack blurted out. "That'll be fine. I'll be there."

This was a chance of a lifetime, the chance to be great. His chance to save the ranch and his dream.

He and Sam quickly planned Jack's trip to Wyoming, "to see how they fit," in Sam's words. "I'm sure we'll be able to work together just fine, though," Sam added. "I've seen you ride, and you're damn good."

The two men said goodbye and Jack hung up, though he kept staring at his phone. He wasn't totally sure this was more than a fantasy.

With Sam as his partner, Jack might be able to finally make some serious money. His old partner was fine, but Sam was a legend. Sam Evans and Jerry Isaacs were top five in the world last year, easy. Arguably number one.

For the first time, he wondered why Sam was no longer riding with Jerry, but dismissed the question quickly. Guys left the circuit for all sorts of reasons, from injuries to old age to just wanting to spend more time with family. A partnership breaking up, even one as successful as Sam and Jerry's, wasn't unusual.

Jack thought again what this could mean for him. A real possibility for his career, a possibility to win, to get to NFR, and maybe even become a champion. With that kind of money, he'd be able to keep the ranch running for the next couple of years, and then he'd be able to retire and start the rodeo school. His heart leaped at the thought.

A chance to fulfill his dream had just dropped into his lap out of nowhere. This could be it, his one opportunity.

He'd need to move to Cheyenne for at least the next couple years, though, and that realization gave him pause. Even though he'd already decided it made sense to move somewhere better suited to the rodeo circuit once the ranch sold, he'd never truly believed he would live anywhere but Spring Valley. And Wyoming was a good long way away.

And of course there was Amy. She would be in California while he was in Wyoming, but what would happen after that? He'd need to talk to her before he found himself so in love with her that he wouldn't be able to give her up if he had to.

Jack tried not to acknowledge the thought that it might just be too late.

As Jack and Tom replaced loose boards and old shelving in the barn, then did the regular work to keep the ranch running, Jack's mind bounced between Wyoming and Amy. After about an hour, Tom straightened and crossed his arms over his chest. "Are you really okay with all this, Jack?"

It took a few seconds for Jack to realize that Tom was talking about putting the ranch up for sale. He had been so preoccupied with Amy and the possibility that they *might* not need to sell after all that his mind had been nowhere near that topic. "Actually," he said, choosing his words with care, "I might have a way to save the ranch if things go right on the circuit this year."

Tom's face fell, and Jack knew he was wondering if Jack expected him to stick around and run the place for another year. "I'm not saying it's going to happen," Jack added hastily, "And I know that if it does, it'll be without your help because you'll be in Boston. I'm just saying that there's a possibility."

He couldn't ask Tom to stick around and run the place. Tom had his own thing to do. Not having anyone to run the ranch made this nearly impossible dream even more difficult, but Jack still couldn't give up on the thought. Not until he'd explored the option completely.

Tom looked skeptical, so Jack said, "I'm not asking anyone to stay on here, or even to stop trying to sell it. It's just something I'm looking into."

This seemed to satisfy Tom, and Jack felt it was time to change the subject. "Tell me about your Boston lady," he said, putting aside his own thoughts to find out more about his brother.

Tom looked awkward for a minute, as if he wasn't

sure about the topic change, but then he couldn't suppress a little smile. "We've been talking for about six months. She's a dental hygienist."

Jack waited patiently, and finally his brother continued. "I can't wait to meet her. She's pretty great. We love each other."

"And you met online?" Jack asked, hoping he only sounded pleasantly curious.

"I know it sounds strange," Tom responded, "but we hit it off really well and we've been calling and texting for months. I know her better than any woman I've ever dated."

Jack slapped his brother on the back. He was happy for Tom. If there was any way Jack could save the ranch, it would definitely need to be done without his brother around, that was for sure. His heart was in Boston.

Jack thought of Amy. His heart was in Spring Valley, but for only a couple more weeks. Where would it go then? Would it be too far away to ever come back to him?

Chapter Eight

Amy shook hands and sat down across from the freck-led, red-haired woman Jose had introduced as Kate. Jose had gone off to find Pop, who was probably hid-ing in the barn now that it was approaching the time for him to meet this woman who might send him into retirement. Amy gave her a smile. "Thanks for com-ing out here. Pop might be a bit of a grump about it, but we all know how hard it is to keep the school run-ning at his age, even if there aren't as many students as there used to be."

Amy tried not to think about the Stuart Ranch sell-ing and giving Pop's school a much-needed influx of students.

Kate waved away the gratitude. "This is as much for me as for him. I've wanted to move for a while now, and Spring Valley seems like the perfect home for me. I just hope I can convince your father that I'm the best candidate."

Amy couldn't help but laugh. "At this point you're the *only* candidate. I'm still shocked Jose managed to arrange this at all."

"Well, I'll do my best," Kate said sincerely.

Amy didn't know what to make of this woman. It wasn't that she didn't like her—she was actually quite sure they could become good friends in no time. It was what she was doing with Jose that was confusing.

She was sweet, honest, pleasant. Jose was loud, constantly kidding regardless of the situation, and could be more than a bit frustrating if you wanted anything other than a good joke. How on earth did they end up together?

"So, how did you and Jose meet?" she asked, hoping she didn't sound like she was prying too much.

Kate gave a little shrug and a smile. "He came by the ranch where I currently work to discuss stock with the owner and we just struck up a conversation. He has a great sense of humor."

Amy nodded. It was definitely true that Jose had a sense of humor. Was that really enough? Before she could ask any other questions, Jose came back into the room. "Pop's sitting at the table. Knock 'em dead," he told Kate. "Not literally, though. He's an old guy and we're not afraid to sue."

Kate laughed and gave a little roll of her eyes to Amy before gathering a few papers from her bag and walking out of the room. Jose took her spot. "What do you think?" he asked Amy.

She didn't know what to say, so she stuck with the most honest thing she could think of. "She seems like a very nice person," she answered.

Jose nodded, though he didn't appear very in awe of her kindness. "Yeah, and she has a great smile. Did you notice? Athletic, attractive, low maintenance. My kind of woman."

Amy doubted Kate would appreciate Jose's list of her most important attributes but said nothing. They were both adults, and who was she to give anyone dating advice?

Speaking of…

She looked at the clock on the wall and her heart thumped hard. "I should go get ready for dinner," she said, standing quickly.

Jose grinned. "That's right, Jack's invited to tonight's meal. You, me, Kate, Jack and the parents. That won't be awkward at all."

Amy pointed a finger at Jose. "It doesn't *have* to be awkward, if you can control yourself and be polite," she warned him.

Jose shrugged in his noncommittal way that drove Amy nuts. "I'll see what I can do," he said.

Amy knew she wasn't going to get anything better from him and left the room, nearly skipping at the thought of what she was going to wear that evening. That morning she'd gone with Cassie for her final wedding dress fitting, and while they were out they'd done a little shopping to fill out Amy's wardrobe. Even though Amy reminded herself again and again she'd be back on the road in a few weeks, she couldn't help but buy a few new pieces of nontravel attire, and she couldn't wait to see Jack's reaction to one piece in particular.

Amy closed her door and smiled at the dress spread out on her bed. Knee length and turquoise blue, the dress was neither very extravagant nor revealing, but it had caught her eye immediately at the store. It was a nearly identical version of her favorite dress from high school, which she'd worn to all their most important occasions: their first date, her eighteenth birthday, graduation, the first time they...

Well, it was a significant part of their history, that was for sure.

Amy dressed and brushed out her hair, laughing every time she looked in the mirror. A decade had fallen away, leaving her the sweet, carefree girl she'd been in high school. And just like back then, she glanced at the time over and over, her stomach a flurry of nerves as she anticipated Jack's arrival.

Once she was ready, Amy went downstairs to talk with Jose and Kate, though she really just wanted to sit at the window and wait for her boyfriend to show up.

Amy wasn't sure if it was just this blast from the past or her finally labeling whatever she and Jack were doing, but she reveled in the word *boyfriend* for a few minutes, even if she'd only said it inside her own head.

When Jose saw Amy, he gave her a big grin. "I know I'm your most beloved brother and pretty much the favorite child around here, but that doesn't mean you need to dress up special every time I come over for dinner, Ames."

She almost stuck her tongue out at him, but she hadn't reverted back to her teenage self *that* much. "I bought a pretty dress today and we're having guests over for dinner, Jose," she explained. "I think that's enough of a reason to look nice."

"Ya hear that, Kate?" Jose said, squeezing his girl-friend's waist with his arm, "Amy already likes you enough to dress nice for you. Isn't that sweet?"

Amy and Kate exchanged amused glances, but be-fore either of them could say anything, Pop entered the room. "Stop teasing your sister and my new em-ployee, Jose, or you'll be eating in the barn with the horses," he grumbled.

Amy gave Kate a big smile. "So, you're moving to Spring Valley?"

Kate nodded with a contented air. "Seems so. I'll be starting mid-November."

Even though that was only a month away, it seemed long to Amy, who had been measuring her life in days since arriving home. By that time, she'd be finishing with the lantern festival in Thailand, her next big ad-venture. After that, who knew where she'd be going?

She could feel her mood start to drop as she thought that far in the future, so she forced her mind back into the present moment. Luckily, Jack chose this moment to drive up in his old truck, and Amy went to the door to meet him out on the porch, someplace private and away from Jose's prying eyes and runaway mouth.

As Jack closed his truck door, he spotted her stand-ing at the top step of the porch, waiting for him, and the look on his face made her blood rush inside her. He walked up to her slowly, a smile playing on the edge of his lips. "Nice dress," he said, looking her up and down slowly.

"Thanks," she responded, sounding out of breath. Something about the way he was sauntering up to her made her lungs stop working correctly. "I bought it today."

"Strange how something brand-new can stir up so many memories," he said, so close now that his voice wasn't much more than a growl reverberating through her body.

Amy could guess exactly which memories he was thinking of, and she could feel herself blushing. She gasped lightly as his arm wrapped around her and pulled her tight to his body, and then his lips were on hers, hard and urgent. She pushed back with all the desire she had to give, kissing him for all she was worth.

When they broke apart, they were both gasping with the rush of electricity, and they kept holding each other tightly, as if they might not be able to stand otherwise. "I know it would be polite to go in and say hi to your folks and all, but I might need a minute before I'm in any sort of condition to do that."

Amy, pressed so close to his body, was well aware of what he meant, and it didn't help her calm down one bit. "Wait here," she said, nearly running the few feet to the door and cracking it open. "Jack and I are going for a short walk before dinner!" she called to Jose, Pop and Kate, who were still sitting in the living room.

Jose gave her a smirk, but the other two behaved as if nothing was amiss, so Amy took it as a good sign and closed the door behind her. She might get some looks from Jose for the rest of the night, but it would be worth it.

Amy's dress wasn't made for the cool evening, but she hardly noticed as they made a beeline for the barn,

Jack's arm wrapped around her waist. Her blood was on fire, and even if it wasn't, there was more than enough heat emanating off Jack to keep her warm whatever the weather.

In the barn, they turned toward one another and kissed again, feeling like the teenagers they used to be who needed to enjoy a few stolen minutes alone whenever they could manage it. Jack's touch on Amy's skin was explosive, and it wasn't long before they were taking full advantage of their privacy.

Afterward, as they resettled their clothing, Jack said, "I don't know if I said this yet, but I *really* like that dress, Amy. I mean, wow."

Amy laughed. "I think it's pretty 'wow' my own self," she replied, falling back into his arms for one more long kiss before they made their way to the door, holding hands.

"Let's just hope Ma hasn't put food on the table yet, or we might be in for a scolding," Amy said as they made their way back toward the lights of the house.

When they passed in front of the large front window, Amy could see Pop, Jose and Kate still talking in the living room, so at least that wouldn't be a problem. As she reached the door, she felt Jack fall behind her, and she turned, curious. He was standing there, looking nervous.

"Is something wrong?" she asked.

"No," he answered, though he didn't move. "It's just—this is kind of a big step, you know. Dinner with the family."

Amy's amusement must've shown on her face, because he nodded as if she'd said something. "I know, I know. I've met your parents a hundred times. Still, this feels serious to me," he explained.

"And that's bad?" she asked, her amusement turning to concern.

He gave her a smile and kissed her nose. "Not bad. Never bad," he said before taking one last breath and walking through the door.

Amy wasn't sure what to make of all that, and something about Jack's manner made her think something had changed since they'd last seen each other, but now wasn't the time to think about it, and she dismissed it as aftereffects of a difficult day preparing the ranch for potential buyers. Soon they were immersed in greetings and introductions between Jack and Kate, and almost immediately Ma called for them to come to the dining room for dinner.

Jose gave Amy several significant glances, but said nothing about her and Jack's disappearance, and nobody else acted at all curious, for which Amy was very relieved, and she settled in to enjoy dinner.

Once dinner was finished and Ma and Pop excused themselves for the evening, Amy sat with Jose, Kate and Jack, unsure what to talk about. Luckily, Kate seemed to have a knack for starting conversations, and she quickly turned her skill on Jack. "I hear you're a roper on the rodeo circuit, Jack. When is your next competition?" she asked, looking at him with wide, curious eyes.

"I'm not sure," Jack answered. Amy expected him to explain that he didn't have a current partner, but instead he turned to look at her as he added, "I might be getting a new roping partner next weekend, so we'll need to see what rodeos are coming up that we can enter."

"You found someone?" Amy asked, curious. When did this happen?

Jack nodded. "I got a call from Sam Evans this morning."

Amy stared at him, amazed. "Sam Evans, one of the best ropers in the country?"

Jack nodded. "He's looking for a new partner. We're going to meet up next weekend, when you're in California, and see if we're a good fit together."

Amy could see the excitement in Jack's eyes, and she grabbed his hand, squeezing it hard. "That's wonderful!" she said.

This could be Jack's chance to achieve his dreams. Be a real big shot on the circuit.

Before Amy could ask any more questions, Jose said, "If you two need to run off for another walk, Kate and I won't stop you."

Kate slapped his arm lightly, looking embarrassed, but it was too late to get back the moment, and soon the conversation turned to other things.

Amy had trouble focusing enough to say much, however. She was bursting with curiosity. If Jack could work with Sam Evans and make some big purses, he'd be able to save the ranch and open his rodeo school. She didn't know what it might mean for the two of them, but she knew it was the best thing for Jack's career.

As JACK DROVE home that night, he felt a strange mix of emotions: he was excited about the new possibilities for being a real contender on the circuit, still euphoric from his and Amy's secret encounter in the barn, content with the pleasant company, stuffed with a delicious dinner. And, though he didn't like to admit it, a little worried.

He didn't know if he and Amy would be able to survive such a fragmented relationship, with her flying all over the world and him in Wyoming and on the circuit, doing what it took to become a champion.

As he settled into his room for the night, Jack opened the drawer of his bedside table and dug into the far back, pulling out a small, ornate box. Sitting on his bed, he raised the lid of the box and looked long and hard at the ring it held inside. The ring that had been waiting in that drawer for ten years.

The ring that had been waiting for Amy to come back to him.

After a long, long while, Jack placed the box back in the drawer and closed it carefully. He would ask her before she left for Thailand. After Brock and Cassie's wedding. By then, he hoped she would be as sure as he was that this was what they wanted.

Even though there were so many things unsettled, he and Amy would be able to sort them out together. As a team. As partners. As husband and wife.

AMY BREATHED IN the cool, wet air. It had rained that morning, and the scent of it was still fresh and sweet. It was hard for her to explain what it meant to be back on a horse again, riding almost daily, and she regretted that she wouldn't be able to see Maverick for the next few days while she was in San Diego and Jack visited Wyoming.

It soothed her soul in a way she'd almost forgotten was possible, and she knew there was no way she could spend another decade away from these amazing animals. Her feelings about Jack were similar, she thought as she looked at him riding beside her. How had she spent a decade without him in her life? His humor, his heart, his eyes, all gave her a feeling of comfort and home. The wall that had built up around her heart over time, girded and strengthened by her experience with Armand, had crumbled a little more each day they were together.

"You up for a race, Ames?" Jack asked, looking over at her with a sideways smile that made her want to lean in to give him a hard kiss.

Instead she winked and gave Maverick the signal to let loose. The horse didn't need much urging, and soon they were flying along the path, Maverick's hooves churning up the fresh ground. Amy let herself savor the moment, the sound of Jack and Benny close behind them, the rush of adrenaline pumping through her.

She tried not to let her worries for the future taint these mornings she spent with Jack, but as each one passed and the number of days they had left together dwindled, she found herself dreading her flight to Thailand.

As much as she told herself they would be able to work out some sort of plan that could keep them together, the logistics of it seemed staggering. If she cut her time out of the States, she would still need to be gone several months of the year in order to make enough money to keep herself afloat.

And then there was Jack on the circuit. If everything worked out on his trip to Cheyenne, he would move there, meaning she would need to give up any time she hoped to spend in Spring Valley so she could be with him.

Amy slowed and looked around. Now that she had found Spring Valley again, her home, it hurt to consider spending as little time there as she had during the past few years.

Jack pulled up beside her and slowed Benny's gait to match Maverick's. "Everything okay, Amy?" he asked, looking at her with concern.

Amy gave him a smile. This wasn't the time to talk about all that. Right now, she wanted to enjoy the time they had together before they parted ways for the next few days. "Just fine. What do you say we go do some roping?"

Jack agreed and they turned their horses toward the paddocks.

JACK WATCHED AMY as Maverick slowly trotted toward the paddock that contained the roping gear. Far too soon for Jack's tastes, the day before his trip to Cheyenne had arrived, and he wasn't ready to say goodbye, even for a couple of days. It felt as if the moment they went their separate ways, everything would change. He tried to tell himself that it was silly, that they would pick up on Monday right where they left off on Thursday. It didn't ease his worries.

As Jack and Amy finished a series of roping exercises, the question that he'd been bursting to ask her since he'd dug out the ring nearly a week before finally became too strong to hold back. He had to know what she was thinking, now, before anything had the chance to change. "Do you think we have a future, Amy?" he asked as they guided the horses back to the barn.

Amy pulled on the reins, stopping Maverick's progress. Jack stopped Benny, too, and they sat looking at each other for a long moment. "I want us to," Amy said, and Jack's heart twisted at her sincerity.

But when she didn't elaborate, he sighed. He'd hoped she would have enough confidence for both of them. "So after the wedding, when you leave…" he prompted.

She shrugged. "We'll keep in contact, and I'll try to fly back a few weeks later for at least a couple of days. I can go out to Cheyenne if that's where you are. After that, we can take it a day at a time."

"A day at a time," Jack repeated.

This wasn't what he wanted to hear, but did it change anything?

Once he proposed, she would come around, he was sure. He loved her, and even though she hadn't said it in nearly a decade, he was sure she still loved him, too.

In silence, they urged Maverick and Benny into the barn. Jack dismounted and started turning toward Amy when he heard her stumble. It was only by the tiniest of margins that he managed to move in time to stop her fall, his arms wrapping around her as her legs folded. "Are you all right?" he asked, looking her over carefully in his concern.

Amy grabbed her head with one hand and his arm with the other, keeping her weight off one ankle. "I think so," she said, though she sounded shaky. "I got dizzy for a second as I was swinging my leg over and landed wrong on my bad ankle."

He watched her put weight on her foot and steady herself a bit. "I'm better now. Just a weird head rush thing, I guess."

Jack looked her up and down carefully. "All the same, I'd prefer if you sit while I take care of the horses."

She really must have been feeling strange, Jack thought, because she nodded and sat down without an argument. As Jack quickly unsaddled and groomed the horses, he kept one eye on Amy, wondering what could make her stumble like that. She'd never been clumsy or prone to fainting spells. Heck, if someone ever implied she couldn't handle herself, they would live to regret it. So to fall while dismounting seemed more than a little weird.

After the horses were both settled in their respective stalls, he came back to where Amy sat. "Maybe you should talk to Cassie about what happened," he said, offering her a hand up.

Amy rolled her eyes and ignored the proffered hand, standing up under her own power. "I don't need to see a doctor for momentary wooziness. I probably just need to drink more water."

Jack wasn't so sure, but Amy really did seem back to normal, so he said nothing about it as he walked her to her father's truck parked in the driveway. "I'll see you for dinner, right?" she asked, and he knew she was thinking of his trip to Cheyenne. He wondered if she felt the same worry he did, that a few days apart might be enough to break whatever fragile thing they had built together over the past couple weeks.

"Dinner," he agreed.

"And before you say anything, I'm fine to drive," she said, giving him a wide grin he knew was at least a little false.

He said nothing and watched her leave, not taking his eyes off the vehicle until it was gone from sight. Even then, he watched the spot where it had been.

He knew he needed to go to Wyoming, that even if he didn't go, Amy would be off to California for the weekend. Still, Jack ached to stay.

AMY DROVE AWAY from Jack's ranch slowly, trying to absorb everything that had happened in those last few minutes, from Jack's question about their future to her near fall. The woozy feeling worried her more than she'd let on, as did the heartrending look on Jack's face when she admitted she wasn't sure about what would happen next in their relationship.

And really, she didn't have a clue what they could do to make this thing between them work. As comfortable as she'd gotten with Jack again, as much as she enjoyed his company and—yes, she could admit it, if only to herself—*loved* him, their lives were so different that the decision to stay together seemed terrifying, whatever her feelings for him.

And in the back of her mind, as much as she hated it, she still kept a little piece of herself hidden from him. She hadn't told him about Armand despite all her promises to herself, and every once in a while, the fear popped up again: the fear that all of Jack's sweetness and affection was a con, that one day not too far from now, he'd show his true colors and hurt her like Armand had.

No matter how often she told herself that it wasn't true, she couldn't entirely rid herself of that feeling.

Amy parked her pop's truck, but hesitated before going into the house. She couldn't do anything at that moment about her relationship with Jack, but she *could* relieve her worries about that moment of light-headedness, and that was better than nothing. Plus, she'd be able to spend a little time with Cassie, which might just make her feel better.

Amy turned her sights on Cassie's house next door and began walking through the scrub grass that sprouted up between the two properties, following a trail most likely worn down by Brock's frequent visits between the houses over the past several months.

As she approached the door, Amy wasn't sure what she planned to say to Cassie besides *I felt dizzy for a minute, what do you think it could be?* She didn't even have enough time for that, however, because the moment Cassie opened the door she said, "Just the person I wanted to see! My dress is steamed and hanging up in the bathroom and I desperately wanted someone to gaze lovingly at it with me. Come in," and Amy was inside and being hauled down the hallway before she could say a single word.

Amy and Cassie both looked at the dress hanging from the shower rod in Cassie's bathroom. It was long and white, with simple, delicate ornamentation. Perfect for a ceremony on the ranch, which Cassie insisted was everything she could ever hope in a wedding. Even though Amy had been with Cassie at her last fitting just a few days before, she couldn't help but look longingly at the dress.

"It's beautiful." Amy sighed, running her fingers along the silky hem.

Cassie's eyes sparkled as she stared at the dress, and Amy could tell she was close to tears. It seemed this was going to be a wedding-themed visit instead of a doctor's visit, and Amy didn't mind one bit.

"When does your family arrive?" Amy asked while they left the bathroom, wondering how big of a part Cassie's mother and sister had in the wedding preparations.

Cassie rolled her eyes. "Oh, you'll know when they get here. I'm pretty sure you'll be able to hear my mom from your parents' house. They fly in a couple days before the wedding."

"Are you...excited to see them?" Amy asked, unsure if she was giving Cassie an opportunity to talk or overstepping her bounds.

Cassie threw her hands in the air in exasperation as she walked over to the bed and sat down. "I have no idea. I love my family, but my mother hasn't always been the easiest person to be around, and I think she's still uncertain about this whole thing. I just don't want to be in charge of corralling her through the entire reception to be sure she doesn't say anything insulting about us deciding to live 'in the middle of nowhere' instead of with 'civilized folks' in the city."

Amy laughed at Cassie's depiction of her mother. She really did sound like quite a handful, and Amy felt a rush of gratitude for her opinionated-but-ultimately-supportive Ma. "Why don't you put Ma in charge of her?" Amy asked as the thought struck. "She'd love a job, and if anyone can convince a person about how great Texas is, it's Ma."

Cassie's eyes lit up at the idea. "That might work," she said, sounding excited. "I can tell my mom that the two of them are in charge of Zach and Carter."

"If Ma gets to be with the twins and browbeat someone into loving Spring Valley at the same time, she might die of happiness. The rest of us will have a hard time following that act," Amy said.

"That's perfect, Amy," Cassie said sincerely. "I'm so glad you came over. Speaking of, I never asked you why you were here. If you were looking for Brock, he and the boys are busy in town for a couple of hours."

"No, I came to see you, actually. I had a weird dizzy spell earlier today and I wanted to check with you about it. You know, as my doctor and all," Amy said, feeling a little silly.

Cassie immediately shifted into doctor mode. "Has this ever happened before? Do you have any other symptoms?"

Amy thought carefully. "It could be period-related, now I think of it. I'm a bit late and my breasts are a little tender. Probably just weird hormones or something. I've never gotten woozy like that before."

"Well, I have one guess," Cassie said immediately.

"I can't be pregnant, Cassie," Amy explained, knowing what Cassie was thinking. "A doctor told me that a decade ago."

Cassie nodded, though she didn't look convinced. "Well, will you take a test for me? That way we can rule it out entirely and move on to other diagnoses."

Before Amy could say anything, Cassie was already back in the bathroom, scrabbling in a cupboard under the sink. After a few seconds, she popped back up with a pregnancy test.

"Whoa," Amy said, "I didn't think you'd have one quite so handy. Are you and Brock planning on growing your family already?"

"I keep some on hand for patient use," Cassie explained, but when Amy didn't break eye contact, she blushed. "But yes, we've talked about giving Zach and Carter a sibling before they get too much older. Now will you go take the test, please?"

Amy took the small object from her soon-to-be sister's outstretched hand. "Okay, but after it comes back negative, will you please let this idea go for now? And really, the whole thing was probably just a weird moment that means nothing. I shouldn't have even bothered you about it."

Cassie held up her hands in promised surrender, and Amy closed the bathroom door behind her. After a minute, she opened the door again, allowing Cassie to reenter the bathroom. The test sat beside the sink. "How long does it take?" she asked Cassie, not even trying to hide her skepticism.

"Just a couple of minutes," Cassie said, looking at her watch.

Amy turned her attention back to the white dress that took up so much of the bathroom. "So, are you hiding this somewhere so Brock won't see it, or are you two not bothering with all that?"

"Oh, we're bothering, all right," Cassie answered. "I was actually hoping we could sneak it over to your place before he and the boys got back from their errands. I'm sure the McNeals would be able to keep it safe, and Ma invited me to get ready over there. I bet if I didn't, she'd be bringing half the house over anyway, just in case we might need something."

Amy chuckled. Ma wasn't about to leave anything to chance for this wedding, Amy was sure of that. Guessing it had probably been long enough by now, she glanced down at the pregnancy test on the counter.

Amy was silent for a long moment before uttering a quiet "Oh."

Chapter Nine

At dinner, Jack watched Amy carefully to see if she was still feeling off from her earlier dizzy spell, and it seemed obvious that she still wasn't feeling herself. He didn't say anything at first, not wanting to make her roll her eyes and insist she was fine. Besides, they were going to be saying goodbye for a few days, and he knew that was enough to make him act oddly.

It seemed silly for a weekend apart to be such a big deal, but it really was. By the time he got back from Wyoming, his career could be back on track, but their relationship might not be able to survive the time and distance that a real shot on the circuit would require.

Finally, though, Jack could tell that Amy was very distracted by something, and it wasn't just her being worried or nervous about the weekend.

"What's going on, Amy? You don't seem like you're actually here with me," he told her, leaning in and grabbing her hand.

For the first time that night, she really seemed to look at him. He waited patiently to see what she'd say.

After a long silence, she finally opened her mouth. "I'm pregnant," she said, in little more than a whisper.

The words rang in his ears as if she yelled them. She was pregnant? How could that be?

"But you can't—" he started, but was unable to finish the sentence.

"I know," she answered, her eyes wide with her own emotions.

He still couldn't make his brain understand what she was saying. "You're—"

"Pregnant," she said again, even quieter.

Then it finally clicked. He broke into a huge grin and pulled her into a tight hug, almost lighting himself on fire when he leaned too close to the candle sitting on the restaurant table. "This is fantastic!" he said, not letting go of her. He couldn't think anything beyond that.

Amy pulled away and searched his eyes with hers. He could see she was barely holding herself together. "Really, fantastic?" she said, shaking her head. "What about you moving to Wyoming and my job and I don't even have health insurance and…"

Her voice drifted off and a tear slid down her cheek.

Jack wiped away the tear with one hand, his palm settling on her neck protectively. "We'll figure it all out, Ames," he said steadily, his blue eyes capturing hers.

He suddenly felt no doubt. Just pure joy. He was finally going to have the family he'd always wanted. Amy and their baby.

"Will you dance with me?" he asked, pulling her onto the dance floor and holding her close, his heart bursting with happiness.

I HAVE TO TELL HIM, Amy thought as they danced, but she couldn't force herself to open her mouth. He was just so delighted that the words wouldn't come out.

It would crush him to hear he might not be the father. This was what he'd always wanted, and the moment she said those words, she wouldn't be able to take them back. So instead she held him close and wished with all her might: *Please, please let this baby be Jack's.*

For the rest of the evening, every time she got her courage up enough that she was about to tell him, she'd see the smile on his face or feel the squeeze of his hand on hers and she would fall silent again. By the time he suggested dessert, she was so exhausted from her internal struggle that she told him she wasn't feeling well—which was true, but not for the reason he thought—and they left shortly after that.

"I wish we could spend more time together this evening, but you probably need some rest, and I have an early flight tomorrow," Jack told her as he settled behind the wheel of his truck.

Amy nodded, but she must have looked anxious, because Jack gave her another big smile. "Don't worry, Ames. I know it seems overwhelming right now, but we'll get everything sorted out as soon as I get back Tuesday."

Tuesday. That was when she'd tell him about Armand and the possibility that he might be the baby's father. She *needed* to tell Jack the truth. But she couldn't tell him right before they parted ways for the weekend. He would have to be at top form if he was going to do well with Sam Evans in Cheyenne, and that was too important to put in jeopardy.

She couldn't tell him this possibly devastating information and risk him being so hurt that he screwed up his chance to pursue his dreams.

After a quick goodbye, Amy was relieved to see Jack leave. She felt guilty about keeping this secret, but it was for the best. Amy sighed and went to her bedroom, but she knew there was no way she'd be going to sleep anytime soon. After a few minutes of aimlessly wandering around the tiny room she opened her laptop and checked her email as a desperate bid for a distraction, hoping she could find something to keep her mind busy.

And she found it, though it wasn't at all what she'd been hoping for.

Amy stared at her computer in disbelief, clicking on the top email robotically, hoping the article wasn't what she thought. The title splashed across the top of the webpage finally brought her out of her stupor and she grimaced.

Married Prince of Monaco Caught in Moroccan Love Affair.

She read the first sentence with mounting disgust.

Prince Armand of Monaco, married father of two, was photographed in an illicit relationship while on a diplomatic visit to Marrakech, Morocco.

After that, she could only skim, unable to read in depth the words that publicized one of the biggest regrets of her life. The tabloid seemed to revel in pointing out again and again that the man in question was married, and the woman an American travel writer by the name of Amy McNeal. They didn't seem very interested in how the woman in question had been duped into thinking he was single and had dumped him as soon as she discovered the truth.

And he could be the father of her child, she thought, appalled. It *had* to be Jack's.

The fact that Armand was a prince only made her annoyed. He'd mentioned his "royal blood" as if she should know what he meant, but she'd been too wrapped up in her loneliness and desperate need for affection to care, and now she only saw it as a cause for this article. If he'd been anybody else, she wouldn't be reading this internet tabloid right now.

As Amy scrolled, she saw with a sinking heart the pictures mentioned in the first sentence. She stared at the photos and groaned, her hand slamming against the desk in anger. Damn Armand and his smooth talk. There were three photos, each one as suggestive as the last. Armand's arm curled around her waist as they ducked into a cab, Armand's lips to her ear as he whispered his beautiful lies, a kiss captured at just the right moment.

Or wrong moment, in Amy's case.

Amy's head filled with if-onlys.

If only she had known he was married.

If only she hadn't been feeling so alone when he approached her.

If only she'd seen through his handsome face and sweet words.

Then her phone buzzed and she read the text, only to add another if-only.

If only Jack hadn't found out this way.

She read the message again:

I'm coming back over. We need to talk.

He had told her on their first date that he'd created a filter to email him when one of her articles posted— it seemed it worked on anything with her name on it. And her name showed up in the article several times, painting her as a sexy seductress. He must've driven home and checked his email to find this piece sitting in his inbox.

He could be coming over for an entirely different reason, she thought, before shaking her head at her own wishful thinking. There was no other possible reason for him to drive back so soon after dropping her off, she was sure of that much.

Amy sent a text back telling him she'd be waiting outside, then steeled herself for whatever might come next.

He'd understand, right? These photos had been taken weeks ago, before they had reunited. Why the tabloid had waited until now to print them, she couldn't say, but they were still before her time with Jack. She was sure he hadn't been some monk waiting for her for the past decade, so he couldn't expect that of her.

But the baby. She hadn't meant to sleep with Armand and then Jack so close together, hadn't *planned* for any of this, and now she needed to come clean and let him know the baby might be someone else's. Would he reject her and the baby in disgust? She couldn't blame him if he did.

Amy stopped the train of thought and walked into the cool evening. No point in arguing against phantom accusations. She needed to give Jack the benefit of the doubt, hope he would take it all in stride.

When his truck pulled up beside her in the driveway, though, Amy's heart sank. Any hope for a sympathetic response to the article disappeared at the sight of his face. She'd known him long enough to be able to tell when he was angry or frustrated but trying to hold it together. From the looks of things, he wasn't managing it particularly well.

Jack held up his phone, the picture of her kissing Armand covering the screen. "What's this about, Amy?" he asked, his voice calm enough that the irritation was only a sharp edge on her name.

"It was before I came home," she said, hoping that would be enough to help him relax. He had to know that, right?

"How long before?" he countered, as if he already knew the answer.

So he'd read the article and done the math. He'd realized she had been seeing Armand almost up until the day she left for Texas. Amy sat down on the gravel and waited for him to say what she was sure would come next.

"How long after you slept with him were you and I together in the barn? Days? Maybe a week?"

He was right, of course, but he didn't even realize the half of it, and it was her responsibility to tell him. Before she could explain, though, he slumped onto the gravel beside her while leaving enough space so they wouldn't touch. "Am I just your rebound while you get over this guy?"

"No!" Amy exclaimed automatically. After a moment, though, she realized that wasn't entirely true. "That first night we were together," she admitted, the words sticking in her throat, "I was still hurting from Armand's betrayal, and I don't know if things would have…progressed so quickly otherwise."

She felt him slump beside her. "But after that," she added quickly, "every close moment we had was just you and me. Armand was gone, and all that was left was my affection for you and my shame that I ever bought into his lies when such a good man was waiting for me here."

He didn't answer, didn't say anything. Didn't even move. So Amy just kept talking, hoping she could say something that would make Jack understand. "Right after I was robbed, I was feeling so alone and unhappy, but I hadn't gotten up the guts to come home. Then this guy comes up to me with his flattering words, and I fell for them out of desperation. I was stupid and he was manipulative. I didn't know he was married at first, and I never realized he was a prince."

Amy paused again, but Jack said nothing. She wanted to look at him, but kept her eyes on the gravel. It was safer at the moment. "We were together for a couple of weeks before his true colors started to show. He was…not a nice guy," she said, knowing she couldn't do justice to the way he'd treated her. "It was only when I found out he was married that I wised up and bought my plane ticket. I flew home the next day."

Jack gave a low whistle, and Amy blushed. She knew Jack had done the math again, and it definitely didn't put her in a good light. This was when she had to say the rest. "And the baby—"

Before she could get out the rest of the words, Jack gasped and threw his face into his hands. It broke her heart to see him that way. "It's not mine," he said, his voice full of despair.

"I don't know," she responded, her voice quiet.

They sat there in silence for a long while, until she couldn't take it anymore. "I didn't plan for it to be like that, you know. I didn't plan for any of this. But I don't want to lose you, Jack."

Her story done, Amy waited.

And waited.

Still, Jack said nothing. Just when Amy didn't think she could take the silence any longer, Jack stood. Amy could hardly see him in the dark, but she watched carefully for any sign of his feelings. He didn't seem angry, but he wasn't looking at her, either. "You should probably get inside," he told her, his voice flat. "It's too cold to be out without a sweater."

"What about you?" she asked, meaning so much in that sentence.

"I just…need time to think, okay?" he answered.

What could she say to that? "Okay," she responded quietly.

"I'll talk to you on Tuesday," he said as he walked to his truck without a backward glance.

Her skin was goosebumped and she'd begun to shiver, but she waited until long after his truck disappeared before she went back inside.

JACK DROVE AWAY, but not toward his family's ranch. Instead, he turned his truck toward open country, driving until he was surrounded by little more than grass and hills.

After a long while, he pulled over and got out of the truck, ignoring the brisk air. He opened the tailgate and sat on it, staring into the darkness that surrounded him.

Amy hadn't cheated on him, obviously, but he couldn't help but feel betrayed. The idea of their first night together being about more than just the two of them hurt. It explained her reaction after, and he could understand what that felt like—if there'd been some way to soothe the pain after she'd disappeared from his life, he was sure he would have jumped at the chance.

He also felt angry at the man that had done all this to Amy. He could feel the embarrassment almost emanating off her as she told her story, though he'd been too wrapped up in his own thoughts to think much about it in the moment. Now, he realized how she must have felt coming back to Texas, her heart and soul battered and broken from first the robbery and then the betrayal from someone she trusted.

Knowing that the baby might not be his, but instead be a product of an encounter with that manipulative liar was a painful blow.

But dammit, that guy would never be the child's parent. Even if he was the biological father, Jack knew Amy well enough to be sure she wouldn't ask the man for a dime. And she was strong enough to raise this kid herself.

But she shouldn't need to. Jack gripped his truck's tailgate and shook his head. Even if the child wasn't his, did it change his feelings for Amy?

That answer was obvious enough. He'd always loved her, had never stopped loving her, and he already loved the child that was half her, even if the other half might not be him. They could still be the family he'd always wanted.

And his last but very real problem was finally clear to him: Would he ever be enough for her, or would he one day come home to find she'd disappeared again, taking her child with her and leaving him alone?

That thought scared him more than anything else.

Jack sighed and lay back into his truck bed and stared at the stars for a long while, ignoring how uncomfortable the cold metal was on his back, trying to figure out what to do next. He could play it safe and break things off with her before it went any further and save himself more pain when it all fell apart somewhere down the road.

But Jack thought of the ring and the baby, and he

knew there was no safe place for him to hide his heart. It was too late for that. Amy and her child already had it, and stopping things now just meant he would miss out on all the possible wonderful moments he might have. The truth was, he wanted that family. So badly that he couldn't imagine running from this opportunity, as complicated as it might be.

Finally, Jack sat up and rubbed his back. There was no question about what he would do, of course. And he needed to let her know before he left for Wyoming the next morning.

Jack got back in his truck and started driving back the way he'd come. When he arrived at Amy's house everything was dark except the living room, which was lit by a single lamp. He could see Amy sitting in the window seat, the light spilling around her, as if she was waiting for him. He rushed out of the truck, and she had just stepped out the front door when he pulled her into his arms, kissing her with all his might.

She kissed back, and they held each other for a long, long time.

AMY SAT ON her bed in the hotel room she and Ma were sharing in San Diego, not sure what to do with herself. Jack was already working with Sam in Wyoming, so she didn't want to bother him, as much as she'd like to call and get assurance once again that he was still a part of her life despite everything with Armand. She had an article to write that she'd been putting off for two weeks, but she doubted she could do much of anything, as distracted as she was. Sitting and doing nothing was only making her feel stir-crazy.

Amy stood up and began pacing. She was having a *baby*. It was still impossible to wrap her mind around it. After all, she'd spent the past decade expecting to never be pregnant. It was just a fact of her life. And now that was turned upside down and here she was with a little one on the way.

Amy wished she felt euphoric about it, like Jack had when he first found out. But instead she felt nervous. And scared.

Now that she had finally accepted the truth of the matter, it left her with so many questions. How would she be able to continue the life she'd created for herself and raise a child? What would the next eighteen years look like? Would she and Jack be able to make all this work?

She didn't have answers to anything, and felt lost. At sea without a life raft. Jack's steadiness and confidence were the only things keeping her afloat, and she had no idea how much longer that might last.

Ma came out of the bathroom shaking her head. "I tell you, dear, this ain't half-bad. The lounge, the airport and now this hotel. Maybe I should convince Howie to see a bit of the world with me."

Amy nodded, though she hardly heard the older woman. After a few moments, Ma came up to her and put a hand on each of Amy's cheeks, staring into her daughter's eyes. "I'll be here for you whatever happens with Maryanne, Amy. Don't you worry."

Amy felt tears welling in her eyes, and she almost

spilled the truth out to her kind adopted mother, but she stopped herself. Ma's entire life had been focused around her children, and Amy just couldn't confess her fears and risk being told to give up everything important in her life for this baby. So she kept silent.

Amy would tell her soon, possibly even before they returned to Texas, but first she needed to sort out her thoughts on her own. Ma patted her cheek gently and smiled encouragingly.

Amy hadn't even been thinking about the reason for their trip to California, and only now considered what it might be like to meet her half sister the next day. As if Amy's phone knew she was thinking of Maryanne, it pinged with a new text message from her:

My son just reminded me he has a birthday party tomorrow at a bowling alley.

Amy's heart sank. They were supposed to meet tomorrow. Was her sister canceling on her again? It didn't seem like she really wanted to see Amy after all. Then the next message showed up:

Are you up for some bowling? I can drop Devin off with his friends and we can get our own lane as far from the party as possible. Your adopted mother is welcome to join, of course.

Amy felt a sense of relief. So Maryanne wasn't begging off from their meet-up. Amy looked over at Ma, who was carefully unpacking her bag into the chest of drawers. "You interested in going bowling with Mary-anne?"

She wasn't sure what she expected Ma's reaction to be, but she certainly didn't expect her to clap her hands with excitement like a child. "I haven't bowled in years!" she exclaimed.

That decided it, and Amy texted Maryanne back. Soon everything was planned and Amy set her phone down. Before she could go back to wondering what to do with herself, Ma was picking up their hotel key card and her purse. "Get up off your behind, dear. We're going to see the ocean."

Amy gave her mother a confused look. "Don't you think it's a bit cold out to go to the beach?" she asked.

Ma shook her head. "I haven't seen the Pacific Ocean in more'n twenty years, and I intend to go right now so we can be there when the sun sets. Grab a sweater so you won't be chilled."

Amy hopped up immediately, threw on her jacket and followed her mother out the door. In no time at all, they were standing on a beach, sitting with their toes in the cold sand despite the temperature, watching the waves crash against the shore.

"I love Texas with all my heart and soul," Ma said quietly, almost as if she was speaking to herself, "but there's something about watching the sun set over the ocean that lifts my spirit. I shouldn't have waited so long to see it again."

Amy said nothing, just watched the rolling waves as the sun touched the horizon. Brock had grown up here, and this place must hold special memories for

Ma and her sister, Jeannie, Brock's mother. It certainly was beautiful, and she loved this time with Ma, but her mind kept drifting back to Jack in Wyoming. If everything worked out there, he would be incredibly busy for months, years even, as he pushed to make it to the top. Even if he wanted to be a part of the baby's life, how could that work?

Even these few hours apart were hard—she couldn't imagine what it would be like when she was in Chiang Mai and he was on the circuit. Even if she loved him and he loved her, she would be very, very alone. Could they make it work without constantly tearing themselves apart?

Amy stared at the water as the sun went down, wishing she had answers to everything. Ma patted her hand, catching Amy's attention. The older woman smiled kindly at her. "Don't you worry, dear. You two will figure it out."

It took Amy a moment to realize what Ma meant. "How did you know what I was thinking?" Amy asked.

"Are you ever *not* thinking about Jack Stuart these days?" her mother responded.

Amy didn't know what to say to that. "Love is difficult," Ma continued. "You will find what's right for you."

Amy wanted those words to reassure her, but she couldn't help but be skeptical. Sometimes things just didn't work out. She knew that well enough.

And wishes couldn't change facts here. She would try to have a lasting relationship with Jack, and they might try to raise a child together, but would it work?

Or would the facts be so strongly against them that wishes wouldn't matter?

The sun dropped below the horizon with a last tiny flash of light and the two women sat in the sand for another moment before standing. "Dinner and then bed," Ma announced as they brushed the sand off their feet. "Tomorrow's a big day."

Amy's heart jumped. Tomorrow she would spend some quality time with her half sister. She would learn about where she came from, at least a little bit. It was time to put Jack and the baby aside for the time being, as hard as that seemed to be, and focus her attention on the here and now.

Chapter Ten

Jack woke early, his eyes bleary from getting so little sleep. With everything on his mind, from his upcoming roping session at Sam's to Amy and the pregnancy, it was hard to quiet his brain enough to rest.

Still, he was satisfied that he'd come up with the best plan for his new family. It would hurt to give up on his dream for the Stuart ranch once and for all, but he'd finally had to admit to himself that he couldn't put every cent into the place, which was what it needed to make it work. No, there was something more important now. The child in his arms would be the only thing that mattered.

He also needed to decide how to propose to Amy. He'd been planning to wait until her trip to Chiang Mai, but with the pregnancy, all that had changed. Putting it off until after Brock and Cassie's wedding seemed silly now.

Jack pulled himself out of bed and splashed some water on his face. He needed to be at his best if he was going to turn these few days with Sam into a lucrative career move, and that was more important now than it had ever been.

A couple of hours later, Jack wiped the sweat from his face. Even though the air was cool, he was burning up. Almost the moment he'd gotten onto Sam's property he'd been put to work running drills, showing his abilities as best he could. Sam was watching him carefully, and Jack felt like everything he did was being scrutinized, and he hoped he wasn't coming up short. He needed this. For Amy. For the baby.

Jack looked around beyond the practice arena he was currently working in. He hadn't yet had a chance to look around the ranch much, but from what he'd seen, it was pretty fantastic. Everything a rodeo cowboy could possibly want. Jack's heart longed for something like this back in Spring Valley, and he could almost picture what he'd need to do to Stuart Ranch to make it a reality. Before he could get too lost in that old pointless dream, though, Sam rode once more to the starting position. "Come on, Jack, let's go at it again. And pay attention this time."

Jack bit his lip and turned his horse toward where Sam was waiting. He was starting to understand why Sam's old partner might've quit. While the man was a great roper, one of the best, he was also a frustrating person to work with. Even after such a short time, Jack could tell that Sam was a rigid taskmaster who spoke to almost everyone with brusque condescension, including his teammates.

It was clear that for this to work, Jack would need to keep his mouth shut and do everything asked of him, no matter his opinion. That would be the only way to set his career on the right path and do what was best for his family.

"Focus, Jack," Sam said, cutting into his thoughts. "I expect better this time."

Sam waved his hand in the air and a steer was released into the arena. Jack gripped his rope and rode in time with Sam toward the animal. In just a few seconds the steer was immobilized and Jack felt a grin of triumph spread across his lips. It had been a great ride, first place in most any rodeo.

Sam pinched his lips together and shook his head as they let the steer loose. "You turned a little slowly at the end there. Wasted a quarter second. Let's try again."

By noon, Jack was exhausted and his nerves were frayed from Sam's constant criticisms. Jack's partners had always been supportive and excited to ride together. They'd been a team but also friends. Sam, however, seemed to be making it very clear that he didn't want a friend.

Jack dismounted and rotated his roping arm slowly, feeling the burn of the muscles beneath the skin. Sam walked over to him and held out his hand. "I think we'll be able to do great things, Jack," he said with a small smile.

Jack shook the proffered hand, though he found it difficult to return the smile. It had been a long work day, and not exactly the pleasantest in recent memory. But this was his chance and he had to take it.

AMY STOOD IN front of the bowling alley, unable to make her feet move. This was the big moment, and now that it was here, she wasn't sure she'd be able to do it. Ma, however, seemed unfazed by the momentousness of the occasion. "Hurry up, dear. For a woman who travels around the world constantly, you move slow as molasses sometimes."

With that, her mother set a brisk pace toward the entrance, and Amy could do nothing but hurry to follow. Inside was dim compared to the bright sunlight, and it took a moment for Amy's eyes to adjust. Before they could, she was engulfed in a hug. "Amy, you're here!" said a woman who Amy couldn't see but assumed to be Maryanne.

The woman stood back and, sure enough, she matched the picture Maryanne had sent. Amy's same nose and mouth set into a different, darker face and surrounded by dark wavy hair. "I'm sorry for attacking you the moment you walked in. I'm just so excited that you're here. Thank you for coming," she added, turning to Amy's adopted mother and grasping the older woman's hand in both of her own.

After brief introductions, the three of them settled into a lane and started lacing their rented shoes. "Thanks for agreeing to meet at the bowling alley," Maryanne said over the din of balls hitting pins. "I would hate to disappoint my son when he'd been looking forward to this for weeks. I can be a bit scatter-brained."

Amy smiled, but before she could say anything, Ma was already reassuring Maryanne. "I think this'll be a hoot, dear," she said as she went to choose her bowling ball.

"Your adopted mother seems wonderful," Maryanne told her while the older woman was out of earshot.

Amy had to agree. "I've been very lucky."

Maryanne seemed to know what Amy was thinking, because she pulled a picture out of her purse. "This," she said, handing one to Amy, "Is our biological mother. She… Well, she's a difficult woman to explain."

Amy stared at the photo, trying to absorb that this was her mother. Maryanne kept speaking, and Amy listened intently. "I don't know much about your adoption, just that Mom was young when she had you and wasn't ready to have a kid. Not that she was much more prepared when I came along a few years later."

Maryanne gave a sad little laugh that tugged at Amy's heart, and Amy squeezed her sister's hand. Maryanne shrugged, as if to say the past was the past. "I bounced between her and my dad a lot when I was little, but didn't see her much by the time I was a teenager. I'm sorry to tell you that I don't know where she is now."

Amy still said nothing, staring at her mother. The woman in the photograph was thin and pretty, with a wide grin, but the characteristic that caught Amy's attention more than anything else was her eyes. Those were Amy's eyes. It was such a strange feeling, holding a picture of the woman who had given birth to her almost thirty years ago, then put her up for adoption.

A loud crash of pins broke Amy's concentration, and she looked up to see Ma standing triumphant as the screen above their lane announced a strike. "Who's next?" Ma asked, sitting down.

"I didn't know you were bringing a ringer to bowling," Maryanne commented before standing.

Amy shook her head. "Me neither," she said.

After several games of bowling, each one ending with Ma soundly destroying the other two women, the birthday party wrapped up and Amy drove to Maryanne's home while Ma went back to the hotel to "rest on her laurels," as she put it.

Amy sat at Maryanne's table as her half sister pulled out a box of pictures and a photo album. "The box is full of random pictures—some from my father's side and some from Mom's, but the album is all Mom and other people related to you. I brought it with me to Texas. I'm still so sorry about that, Amy."

Amy waved away the apology and opened the album. Her mother stared out at her from the pages, looking young and happy in most of them. She looked friendly and outgoing. Amy turned to Maryanne, remembering the way she'd spoken about their mother at the bowling alley.

"Tell me about her," Amy said, pointing to the woman in the pictures.

Maryanne sighed. "She…loves her life. Every time I was around her, she'd tell me about the things she was doing and the exciting people she'd met. And she was very extroverted, always the life of every party."

Amy waited a moment, but Maryanne seemed reluctant to go on. "But…" she prompted, knowing that would be the next word out of Maryanne's mouth.

"But she didn't really want children, and I always felt like more of a hindrance than an actual part of her life. She didn't have the time or patience to care about anyone but herself, and she was flighty. Here one day, off on her newest adventure the next without a word of warning. We lost touch when I grew old enough to resent it and stopped pushing us to have a relationship."

Amy took in all this information, staring at the photos in front of her. Their mother hadn't wanted a child, hadn't been prepared for a child, and Maryanne suffered because of it. Amy felt a twinge of fear run through her. Was she going to be like her mother in that way?

Maryanne turned the page and pointed out an older woman, explaining that it was their grandmother. Amy could hardly listen.

After a few more minutes, Amy left her sister's house, thanking her for the information, but insisting she needed to go. Maryanne gave Amy a concerned look. "I'm sorry if I've said anything that upset you. I really would like us to have a relationship, Amy."

Amy hugged Maryanne and assured her that they would stay in contact, and then she hopped into her rental car and drove toward the hotel. Once she was parked in the lot, however, she didn't make a move to leave the vehicle.

The truth about her biological mother worried Amy more than she liked to admit, and she couldn't seem to get it out of her head. All her fears about her ability to be a good parent while still living her life and traveling shot to the surface. Would she end up having the same kind of relationship with her son or daughter as Maryanne experienced?

Maybe it wasn't worth the risk. Maybe setting up an adoption with a good family before the baby was even born would be the best thing for everyone involved.

Jack would be devastated, she knew. He would never forgive her for ruining his chance to have the dream family he'd always wanted. But, Amy reminded herself, that dream was unrealistic anyway. It didn't include her job taking her out of the country or him being away on the rodeo circuit for months at a time. What he had was a vague wish that couldn't possibly match up with the reality of their lives.

Perhaps it was better to hurt him with the truth now.

Amy shook her head in exasperation. She didn't know what to do and it frustrated her to no end. Before she'd come back to Spring Valley, life was simple. Even if she didn't know where she was going to be in two weeks, she didn't worry about it. Now she was panicking over events that wouldn't occur for eight months or more.

Amy sighed and finally climbed out of the car, walking mechanically toward the hotel elevators.

When she arrived back at their room, Ma looked uncharacteristically nervous. "How did it go?" she asked, almost timidly.

Amy shook her head, unable to explain.

Ma said nothing, just walked toward her adopted daughter and pulled her into a tight hug. Amy hugged her back, all her panic and worries crashing on her like waves at the beach, one right after the other. In a whisper, she said, "Thank you, Ma. For giving me a home and a family."

Ma hugged her with all her might.

JACK WAITED IMPATIENTLY with his phone to his ear, wanting so badly to hear Amy's voice on the other end. After the day he'd had with Sam, he needed a bit of a pick-me-up, and this phone call was sure to be that if it went the way he expected.

"Jack," she said, her voice almost a sigh.

"Hey Ames," he answered, feeling suddenly relaxed, at ease. He loved the sound of her voice.

"How's Wyoming?" she asked.

"It's great," he told her, trying to put enthusiasm into his voice.

He had already decided not to tell her about Sam's difficult personality. It was something he would no doubt get used to after a couple weeks, and she was already worried enough without his adding more to the pile. His job at the moment was all about easing her doubts, not adding to them.

And he was bursting with news on that front. "Amy, I found us a house," he blurted out, excited to share the news.

"A house?" she said, sounding unsure.

He'd known she would react like that—after all, they'd never talked about a house before. He launched into an explanation. "Well, a neighborhood, really," he said. "I don't have the money right now, but once the ranch sells and I make a couple big purses we'll have enough for a down payment. We'll need to rent until then."

He waited for a reaction, but there was only silence from the other end of the line, so he continued, "It's in the suburbs of Cheyenne, near to Sam's ranch. The whole area is filled with three-bedroom tract homes, just the thing we'll need for a family."

He smiled to himself, sure he'd just eliminated so many of their problems. With a home all their own, Amy and the baby would be settled and comfortable while he was on the circuit, and he'd have a place to come back to. They could start living the life they needed to live.

Amy finally spoke, her voice hesitant. "I thought you wanted to save the ranch and put all your money toward the rodeo school," she said.

Jack grimaced. "I hate giving up the ranch, but it's the only way I can get enough money together for the baby."

He could tell she was dwelling on the loss of the rodeo school, and it was starting to dampen his spirits. He wanted her to be excited about all this.

"How about you come out here with me after Brock and Cassie's wedding? You can look at the houses first-hand, and if the ranch gets an offer by then, maybe we'll be able to make one of our own," he told her.

"I'm going to Thailand after the wedding. My flight's a couple days later. I won't have time to go to Wyoming," Amy told him.

Jack knitted his brows. "Is your ticket nonrefundable? If you call the airline and tell them you're pregnant, maybe they'll waive the cancelation fees."

"No, I have trip cancelation insurance. I wasn't planning on canceling it."

"You weren't?" Jack asked, genuinely surprised. "But you're pregnant. Don't you need to stay home and go to doctor's appointments, relax, that sort of thing? Aren't you worried about going to Thailand and catching some kind of bug that might affect the baby?"

Jack was incredulous. It was as if Amy didn't understand that everything had changed.

"So I'm supposed to turn my entire life upside down because I miraculously got pregnant a couple weeks ago?" she asked, sounding angry.

Jack wished they were having this conversation in person instead of over the phone. He would be able to explain it so much better in person. "Well…yeah," he said as calmly as he could. "This is our family, Ames." He willed her to understand how important this was.

"I need to go pack for my flight" was all she said in response.

Before he could say anything else, she was gone. He briefly considered calling her back. But what would he say? It was best to let her calm down and see reason, and when he was back in Spring Valley the day after tomorrow, they could talk about it again. She'd have a clearer head by then.

AMY STARED AT the phone, shaking her head. How could Jack sacrifice so much, his ranch and home and dreams, for a tiny little baby who wasn't even born yet?

Was she the one who was being ridiculous in this situation?

It bothered her to think that might be true. Her conversation with Jack seemed to be one more example that she was too much like her biological mother.

But maybe she could fake it. Go to Wyoming and live in a nice house in the suburbs. Do all the mom things. And maybe someday she'd find a way to be happy living that life.

Really, what were her alternatives?

After sitting and thinking for a long time, Amy opened up her laptop and looked up her airline ticket to Thailand. After only a last brief hesitation, she moved her cursor over the words "Change/Cancel Reservation" and clicked.

Chapter Eleven

The moment Amy stepped out of Pop's truck back at the ranch, she made a beeline for the neighboring house. She knocked on the large wood door, praying Cassie would be the one to open it. She loved Brock, but didn't think she could face her big brother right now.

To Amy's relief, her sister-in-law opened the door, took one look at Amy, and folded her into a hug. It was exactly what Amy needed, and she grasped onto Cassie with all her might. When they finally let go, Cassie led Amy inside the door and shut it. "Do you need a doctor's office or a sister's shoulder?" she asked.

Amy laughed a little. "Sister, though I do feel like I'm going to throw up."

Cassie nodded and rushed off for a moment, asking her to wait there. Seconds later, Amy could hear Brock and the twins leaving the house through the back door in a noisy storm of boots and voices. Then Cassie was back, ushering Amy into the kitchen. "I sent the boys out for a while so we could have our privacy. Something to drink?" she asked, moving to the cupboard.

Amy shook her head, but Cassie was already pouring hot water into a mug. Soon Amy had a cup of tea on the kitchen table in front of her, and she grabbed it with both hands, as if the heat could rid her of some of her swirling emotions. "It's ginger tea," Cassie said, "so it should help with the nausea."

Amy nodded her thanks and took a sip. "I'd prefer a rum and Coke, but considering the situation, this is perfect. Thank you."

Cassie sat down across from Amy with her own cup and waited quietly while Amy drank another sip of tea. "Did something happen at your sister's?" Cassie asked when Amy put the cup down.

Amy shrugged. She didn't want to get too much into what she had learned about her biological mother. "I came over to tell you I won't be at your wedding. I'm so, so sorry, Cassie."

Cassie looked stricken, and Amy flushed with embarrassment. "You won't be there?" Cassie asked, sounding so upset that Amy had to bite her lip to keep from crying.

"I changed my flight to Thailand. I'm leaving first thing in the morning. I just need to get out of the country," she said.

"Before Jack gets back from Wyoming," Cassie said, a statement rather than a question.

If Amy hadn't already been blushing, she would have done so now. She felt the heat emanating from her face. "If I see him, I'll cave," she whispered.

She knew she would, too. She'd never be able to hold out against his determination to do what he thought was best for her and the baby. He would convince her to move to Wyoming and then what? She'd spent the last decade making a life for herself, and then she'd just throw it away. And if she regretted it in one or two or five years, what would she do then?

No, she needed to leave again. Jack would be able to pursue his dreams and she… Well, she'd need to figure out what she was going to do next.

"I wish you wouldn't go," Cassie said, breaking into Amy's thoughts.

Amy stood. She needed to get to her room, where she could lie on the bed and privately cry for all she was leaving behind. Even though she felt this was the better choice for both Jack and herself, the thought of giving up her chance with Jack was killing her.

Ma's reaction hadn't helped any, either. The older woman was devastated. Amy couldn't bring herself to explain why, not when she was still so confused about what to do with this pregnancy and everything. She wanted to curl up like a child in Ma's arms and hear her comforting words, but she and Pop had gone out to dinner, most likely as a chance for him to talk her out of her depression at their daughter's sudden decision to leave without warning.

Once Amy left Cassie's house, giving her sister one last hug and trying not to notice the tears in the other woman's eyes, she went home and curled up in her bed, alone. It was only then that she let herself cry. She cried for the future she and Jack could have, the poor baby that didn't ask for any of this, and a dozen other things. She fell asleep with tears on her eyelashes.

On the airplane the next morning, there were no more tears, but Amy still felt raw and tired. She tried to blame it on the pregnancy, but she knew it was more about the decision she'd made. She told herself over and over that if she wanted Jack to pursue his dream instead of settling for a house in the suburbs, she needed to force his hand the only way she knew how. As much as it killed her, they couldn't stay together and both be happy, so it was up to her to keep them apart.

Even so, she felt incredibly selfish. Whatever she said, she knew that she was leaving mostly because of her own fear, her own desire to keep the life she knew and loved.

Amy willed the plane to move faster, to get her to Thailand. Maybe if she was far enough away and surrounded by a world different enough from her own, she'd be able to forget the way Jack's cornflower blue eyes sparkled when he smiled at her.

JACK AWOKE WITH a warm feeling of expectation running through him. Soon it would be time to catch his flight, and then he'd be in Spring Valley, where Amy was waiting for him. Even though their last phone conversation hadn't gone the way he'd wanted, Jack knew that a good talk in person would sort everything out, and before too much longer, they would be moving into a house together in Cheyenne, settling down and preparing for the arrival of the baby.

The image brought a smile to Jack's face, and he let

himself enjoy it for a few more moments before getting up and packing his things that he'd scattered around the tiny room where he'd been staying the past few days.

Normally he was a somewhat tidy person, but the rigor and demands of working with Sam Evans, along with spending every spare moment searching around the area for a decent place to rent and various other details that came with moving to a new place, had made him careless, and things were scattered everywhere.

He was relieved to be leaving Wyoming, not just because he was excited to see Amy and his home, but also because he was ready for a break from Sam. The man had only gotten more harsh and constantly critical once they'd agreed to be partners, and working with him was more difficult than Jack had imagined. He was sure they'd settle into each other's personalities eventually, and once they won a few purses together, Sam would probably calm down a bit.

Jack looked around the room, ensuring he hadn't missed anything, then checked the time on his phone. He still had a few minutes before he needed to leave, so he sat to glance through his email. One message caught his eye first. Something from Amy. He opened it.

I'm going to Thailand, Jack. My flight leaves at 6am, so I'll be gone before you get back to Texas. I need some time away. I want you to have your rodeo school and your dream, and I don't think that's possible with me in your life.

I'm sorry.

That was it. Jack couldn't believe it. It was past seven already, but he called her phone anyway, just in case this was some kind of a mistake.

No answer. She'd really left him again. Jack slumped forward, not sure what to do next.

After a two-hour flight that seemed to take forever, Jack went straight to Amy's parents' house. He refused to believe she had really gone until he saw proof for himself.

As soon as Amy's mother opened the door, though, he knew it was true. The woman looked so crestfallen that she didn't need to say anything. "She really left," he said, mostly speaking to himself.

The woman nodded. "Would you like to come in, Jack?" she said, her voice soft and sounding as though she had a cold.

Jack shook his head. He needed to be alone, away from everything that screamed out Amy's absence. He got back into his truck and drove away, hoping a long drive would soothe his anger and sadness, but even his truck smelled faintly of her. Soon he was walking along a dirt road, trying to get as far from Amy as he could.

Like a ghost, she followed him.

Jack sat in the dirt, unable to go any farther. She'd run away from him again, just as he'd feared she would. And now he didn't know what to do. He was sure he couldn't just forget about her, or about the baby that he planned to raise, but what could he do? He couldn't force her to allow him into her life.

Finally he drove home. He didn't know what he would do there that could keep his mind off all this, but he hoped to find something better than just sitting around thinking.

As soon as he walked in the door, though, it became clear he wasn't going to be done with the topic anytime soon. His mom was sitting in the front room, and it was clear she'd been waiting for him.

"I'm guessing you heard," he said, sitting down heavily on the couch.

She leaned toward him. "I spoke to her mother today. I know this must be very difficult for you, Jack."

Jack shrugged. He didn't want to talk about it. Of course it was difficult. He felt abandoned. Rejected. Betrayed.

Again.

"I know there's nothing I can do to help," his mother continued, "But I hope you can find some way to move past this. You deserve someone who won't run away from you when things get difficult, and I know she's out there somewhere."

With that, she patted his knee and stood, leaving him to his thoughts. After a few minutes, Jack stood and stalked to his room, his bewilderment and pain turning into anger. He walked directly over to his bedside table, grabbed the ring box sitting on top of it and dropped it back into the back of the drawer where he'd found it, shutting the drawer so hard that the lamp on top nearly toppled off.

Jack knew what he needed to do. He needed to pack

and get ready to leave for Wyoming. It was time to get the hell out of Spring Valley.

AMY BRACED HER body as the open-back truck careened around a corner, the driver apparently trying to hit every pothole he could find. *If riding horses is bad for pregnant women, I can't imagine this is good,* she thought.

Amy banged on the window to get the driver's attention and hopped out, even though she could still see her hotel behind her and was nowhere near her next destination. After a short argument and paying the equivalent of about fifty cents, Amy watched the red truck continue down the street, followed by three similar vehicles. Amy pulled out her phone, hoping one of her car service apps would work in this country, since the taxi system apparently left a lot to be desired.

A couple of months ago, a bumpy ride on a bench bolted into the back of a truck would be hardly worth noticing except as an interesting cultural phenomenon, but now things were different. There was a baby to think about.

An image of Jack's silver truck, old but with an unmistakable feeling of security built into it, enveloped her, and she longed for home. Amy could feel tears prick her eyes, and it was difficult to see her phone screen for a minute. Finally, she was able to request a car to pick her up, and she leaned against a wall while she waited for it to arrive, trying to stay out of the sun.

The moist heat of the air filled her lungs, and she

wished for a cool rain. Like the one that had trapped her and Jack in the barn after their "first date."

Amy bit her lip in frustration. She had been in Chiang Mai for twenty-four hours, and she'd spent almost all of that time wishing for Jack and home, or else feeling nauseated and wanting food from home, which was so completely different from the ubiquitous Thai offerings that she'd already broken down and visited a Mexican restaurant for food that tasted exactly like she should've expected food at a Mexican restaurant in Thailand to taste like.

Amy stopped the flow of negative thoughts and tried to pull herself together. Since when did she complain so much about the little difficulties that came with travel? She was here to have adventures, experience a new culture and see the lantern festival, something she'd wanted to do for years. Then she would write an article about it and get paid. Anyone would love to have this opportunity.

It upset her to no end that she was absolutely miserable.

Before she could dig into everything that had changed and what that meant for her, Amy's ride, a sleek black car stopped in front of her and she hopped in, determined to at least give this city a chance. She directed the driver to the temple she had planned to visit, then leaned back against the cushions and soaked in the air conditioning. Without thinking, her hand crept to her stomach, as if she could feel the child growing inside her.

The child whose future depended completely on her

decisions, even though she felt more lost and confused than she ever had in her life. She didn't feel like she was remotely capable of making decisions for anyone, let alone an innocent baby.

Amy repeated the mantra she'd started as soon as she arrived in Thailand: If she could just make it to the lantern festival, everything would sort itself out somehow. She knew it was illogical, stupid even, to assume that she would magically know what to do after that, but she had to hold on to some sort of hope. Unfortunately, the lantern festival was weeks away still, and Amy had no idea how she would survive until then.

But this was her life, right? If she wasn't willing to give it up for Jack and the baby, then she better find some way to enjoy it.

Maybe by the time the festival was over and she moved on to the next place, her heart would hurt less. Then she could broach what to do about this baby. Right now, she missed Jack so deeply it was hard to think about much else. After two weeks, hopefully she would have healed enough to think about life without Jack and not feel pain.

Amy tried to believe that, but couldn't quite manage it.

She arrived at the temple and walked past the statues and worshippers half-heartedly, taking pictures and notes for her article, but not actually seeing much of the scene before her. Her thoughts were so focused inward that it was impossible for her to do much more than wander aimlessly. Finally, she sat down on a bench in the shade as out of way as she could find and sighed.

What was she doing? Where had the spark of adventure gone?

Amy didn't know, and that scared her. She pulled out her phone and glanced through her email, hoping Jack had written back to her. She wanted so badly to hear from him, even if it was an email telling her off. Anything written by him would be a comfort in its own way. But there was nothing from him, not a single word. There was, however, another message that made her sit up. It was from a website editor she'd written for several times, the subject line Important Opportunity, Respond ASAP.

Amy opened it. She read it through once, then again.

Hi Amy!
I saw those pictures of you in The Sun—seems like you're having an exciting time out on the road! I was actually trying to figure out a writer for a series we want for our site: Winter in the Alps. We'd want write-ups of at least four different locations, details about the skiing opportunities and holiday festivities, etc. etc. This could be anywhere from four to as many as ten articles, if you can make them unique enough, and if anybody can do it, it's you. We'll pay expenses and your usual fee per article. Please let me know if you're available and interested as soon as you can!

Amy leaned back and closed her eyes. This was an amazing offer for her, an opportunity to go to a great location with a sure purchaser for her articles about it. And it killed her that she wasn't at all excited about the prospect.

It wasn't just the pregnancy, either, and she knew it. She could easily find doctors in Swiss hospitals for checkups, and she didn't *need* to ski to write about the slopes. She should be jumping at the chance to take this job, baby or not. And now that she'd broken things off with Jack, there was nothing holding her back. How could she say anything but yes?

She closed the email, not sure how to answer.

As Amy sat there, watching the temple-goers pass, there was one person she wanted to speak to, one woman whose advice and voice she most wanted to hear.

Her mom.

Not the biological one—the mom that had gone to every track meet and junior rodeo competition, who'd bought her prom dress, and who'd cried every time she left home.

Amy tapped her phone a few times before putting it to her ear. It rang several times before Ma answered with a very sleepy "Who on earth is calling at this hour?"

Amy almost slapped her forehead. It had to be after midnight in Texas. "Sorry to call so late, Ma," she said.

The voice on the other end suddenly sounded much more alert. "Amy? What's wrong? Did something happen?"

"No, nothing happened," Amy said in her most reassuring voice. "I just forgot about the time difference. I'll call back at a better time."

"Oh, no, dear," Ma said, and Amy could hear her moving around. "I'm awake now, so I expect you to talk to me for a good long bit. Make getting up worth it. What's bothering you, dear?"

Amy smiled. She was sure that Ma wouldn't rest until she found out why Amy had called. "There are a few things going on that I haven't told you about, Ma," she confessed.

At first, Amy had only planned on telling her about Jack and the pregnancy, but as soon as she started everything poured out: the robbery in Morocco, her affair with Armand, her fears about being like her biological mother. All of it. By the time she was finished, tears were streaming down her cheeks.

Her mother was silent on the other side of the line for several long seconds after Amy finished. Then she said, "Oh dear, you *have* had a difficult time of it lately, haven't you?"

Amy laughed through her tears.

"How can I help with all this, Amy?" Ma asked, her voice earnest.

Amy shrugged even though she knew the other woman couldn't see the gesture. "I just needed you to know. I've never felt so lost. Should I move to Wyoming? Keep traveling? Give up the baby or keep it? This is all so confusing."

"Do you remember that book you read in high school, *The Bell Jar*?" Ma asked.

"I remember it," Amy answered, with no idea how Ma was planning to connect this to her life.

"Do you remember the fig tree thing?"

Amy's class had spent almost a week talking about that part of the story, and Ma's meaning became clear in a flash. "She sees her life as a tree and all her different options as figs on it, but she can't decide which thing to pursue," Amy said, digging the scene out of her memory. "Because she doesn't pick one, the options wither and fall around her as she starves."

"Good girl," Ma said. "I can't choose for you, but I can tell you that you best make a choice. Don't wait until it's too late."

Fear still held Amy back. "I'm so scared I'll be a bad mother," she admitted, almost in a whisper.

Ma's voice came to her like a warm hug. "Sweetie, if you're so worried, you'll do just fine. It means you care and you want the best for your baby, and that's what being a good mom is all about."

After another few minutes, Amy hung up the phone and used her app to request another car. Since she had a few minutes to wait, she settled back on the bench, trying to get comfortable.

Her mom was right—she needed to make a choice. It was time to grow up and stop acting on momentary whims and selfish desires that just made her more miserable in the long run.

So what did she really, truly want, for herself and her baby and the other people around her? Amy closed her eyes and created images of her future, trying to assess her feelings about each one. An image of her in a Swiss ski resort, taking pictures and writing articles as it snowed outside, an image of her in Spring Valley with her family, an image of her in Jack's arms, the background a mystery. The baby in her arms, the baby being taken away to another family.

In all that mess, all those lives she could live, what did she want?

Amy opened her eyes and sat up. As afraid as she might feel, or unsure or whatever, she knew what she wanted. And now it was time to put it into action.

Then she stood and went to meet the car waiting for her, hurrying her steps a little. She needed to get back to her hotel room and her computer—she had some flights to book.

JACK SLAMMED ANOTHER bag into the back of his truck. He wasn't sure what was in it, and frankly, he didn't care much. He just needed to get the stuff into the vehicle so he could get out on the road and away from this damn town as quickly as he could.

The past two days, ever since he'd arrived home and learned that Amy was actually gone, had been a blur of cramming everything he owned into duffel bags and working as much as he could on the ranch. His body desperately needed a rest, but he couldn't manage to sit still. It was better to work and keep his mind blank, stay angry. If he wasn't angry, he'd be hurt, and he couldn't deal with that anymore.

As he tossed the last two bags in with the others, Jack heard a truck turn into the driveway. He turned and felt as if he was hallucinating. Amy pulled up beside where he stood, stepped out of the truck and ran toward him. Without thinking, he opened his arms wide and caught her up in them, holding her close.

She was here, back in Spring Valley, back in his arms. He didn't know how or why, and for the moment he couldn't think of anything beyond the feeling of her in his arms. "You left," he said, trying to process what was happening.

Amy nodded, not removing her face from where it rested against his shoulder. "I got to Thailand and realized the only place I wanted to be was wherever you were. Here or Cheyenne, a ranch or in the suburbs. As long as I'm with you, Jack."

He squeezed her close, trying to absorb her words. She continued speaking, her voice a little muffled by his shirt. "I'm not scared anymore, Jack. I know that I love you and I want to have this baby with you."

Jack held Amy tight for another second before forcing his arms to break their hold on her. Amy backed up a little and looked into his face. Her cheeks were stained from her tears. "I love you, Jack," she said again.

"I love you too, Amy," he told her.

She stepped closer, but he moved back, keeping distance between them. He felt so much pain in his heart that he had to stop himself from rubbing the skin above it. He focused on his anger instead.

Her expression grew confused as they looked at one another. He knew what he needed to say next, but it took him a moment to get out the words. Angry, he reminded himself. He was angry. "But I can't do this, Amy."

Shock flooded her face and Jack looked away. He needed to say it all. "When you left the first time, it about killed me. And this time…well, I just know I can't put myself through that again. It's too hard. I love you and I'll always love you, but I can't risk my heart like that."

"I won't run again," she said, her voice a whisper.

Jack shook his head, holding tightly to his fury. "I can't let myself believe that." He thought of his mother's words. "I deserve someone who I know won't disappear when things get difficult, Amy."

He stopped talking, but Amy said nothing else. "I still want to be a part of the baby's life and help any way I can. I'm happy to be your friend, Amy," he said stiffly, knowing it didn't sound sincere.

But it was all he was capable of at the moment, dammit.

Jack finally risked a glance up and felt his anger dissolve in one quick swoop. She wasn't crying, but her expression spoke of the agony she felt. Jack wanted to say something to help, but there was nothing left to say. He knew what he'd said was right. Now he just needed to get away before he caved.

Jack gestured to his full truck and where Benny was waiting nearby, ready to settle into the horse trailer for the long ride to Cheyenne. "I better go. I'll see you at the wedding, Amy."

With that, he turned and walked away, not risking a backward glance until he heard her truck driving away. Once he did, however, he watched until it disappeared, only able to keep himself from chasing after her with the hardest effort.

When she was gone, Jack turned again and continued walking toward where Benny was waiting for him. He hugged the horse's neck tight for a moment, telling himself he'd made the right choice no matter how horrible it made him feel at the moment.

Benny snorted in commiseration. Or maybe in disappointment. Jack couldn't be sure.

Chapter Twelve

Cassie opened the door, nearly squealing in her excitement when she saw that Amy was on the other side. "You're back!" she shrieked as she gave Amy a giant hug. "This means you're going to be here for the wedding, right?" she asked, leaning away and looking into Amy's face.

Amy nodded, but Cassie's face fell immediately. "What happened?" she asked, looking concerned.

Amy felt the tears she'd managed to suppress at Jack's coming to the surface, but she held them back. This was a time to stop being so selfish. Cassie was getting married in a week, and she deserved Amy's attention, not Amy's sadness and tears. "It doesn't matter right now. What matters is that I shouldn't have left. I'm sorry for the way I treated you, and if you don't want me to be your bridesmaid, I understand."

Cassie pulled Amy into another hug, this one full of sympathy instead of excitement. "Of course I want you to be my bridesmaid. You're my sister," Cassie said.

In a flash, the two women were inside, sitting at the kitchen table. "You sure you don't want to tell me what's wrong?" Cassie asked again, looking into Amy's eyes.

Amy wanted to sob into her sister's shoulder about her heartbreak and shame at causing a sweet man like Jack to feel so hurt and angry, but she held it all back. "I've just made a lot of mistakes the past couple of weeks—years, actually—and they're coming back to me," she said, chiding herself. Before Cassie could say anything, Amy added, "But I'm going to try to be better. I want to be a stronger, more selfless person. For my baby, if nothing else."

Cassie gave her an encouraging smile. "It sounds like you did some soul-searching in Thailand."

Amy tried to smile, but failed. "You could say that."

Amy wanted to curl up and cry about Jack, beat herself up over all the pain she had caused him with her selfishness, and mourn the loss of the man she loved. Now that she'd said what she needed to and apologized to Cassie, her strength felt sapped. She stood up slowly. "I should get home," she said.

Cassie stood and grabbed Amy's arm. "I don't know what happened, but I'm here if there's anything I can do to help. Same with Brock. And your entire family."

Amy nodded, though she hardly heard the words, and walked out and toward her parents' house. It was only when she was at the midpoint between the two ranches that Cassie's words really sunk in. She had so much family and so much love around her. She needed to remember that.

When she arrived home, Amy fell into Ma and Pop's arms, apologizing for her disappearance. Then she told them about what happened with Jack. "You were right,

Ma," she said at last. "I didn't make the choice I really wanted, and by the time I realized it, I was too late. I've lost him."

Pop shook his head. "Are you going to give him up that easy, Amy?"

Amy looked up at her father, not sure what he meant. Her mother nodded in agreement. "Why, if I had let Howie go when he told me I was too stubborn to date, you wouldn't be sitting on this couch with us," she said.

Amy looked to Pop in surprise. He nodded and wrapped his arm around his wife. "She convinced me to give her another chance, and I haven't let her go since. I just thank my lucky stars she was smart enough to see what I couldn't't."

Amy had to smile at the couple. They'd been married for nearly forty years, but they were looking at each other like newlyweds.

When Amy went to bed that night, she felt a new emotion: determination. She wouldn't give Jack up just yet. She had to try once more, give it another shot. If he still didn't want her, she would accept his decision, but she wasn't going to throw up her arms and let him go without a fight.

Now she needed to figure out what she could do to prove to him that she was in for the long haul, and it better be good.

"Dammit, Jack, pull it together!" Sam yelled across the paddock.

Jack took a deep breath and looked down at the rope in his hand. He was just a second too slow, a second off, but it was enough. The difference between winning and losing.

And Sam wasn't going to let that slide. He rode up to Jack, getting close enough to his face that Jack leaned back, away from him. "I don't know what your problem is, Jack, but you need to pull it together. I expect to win this year, and if you don't, you should just get the hell out of here."

Jack bit his tongue, holding back the torrent of words. Sam was the best there was, and it wouldn't do to piss him off any more than Jack already had. Instead, Jack turned Benny to get back into position. "Let's do it again."

They went through the process again, but Jack's throw was even worse than before.

"What are you doing, Jack!" Sam yelled, throwing his hat to the floor.

Jack watched as Sam's face turned red, but he forced himself to remain calm. He'd already learned not to react to Sam's little tantrums or they only got worse.

To be fair, Jack was a little frustrated with himself, too. For the past couple of days he'd been missing throws he could make in his sleep ever since he was a teenager. His mind was somewhere else, and it was driving Sam crazy.

"If you don't want to be here, you damn well better not come back after that wedding, Jack. I expect to win a purse in two weeks, not be a laughingstock. And with you throwing like you are today—"

Sam stopped talking and turned his horse. He rode away, still seething.

Jack didn't say anything, just sat on Benny and watched Sam ride away. He was sure if he said any of the thoughts swirling in his mind, it would mean the end of his time working with Sam already, and he didn't want that. Sam was the way to the top. If he could pull together his own performance, of course.

It was no surprise to Jack that he was roping so badly. It seemed like the closer it got to the wedding, the worse he got. And with the wedding the next afternoon, this was by far his worst session yet. He was glad he'd be leaving in a couple hours, if only to get away from his terrible riding.

He would be seeing Amy again, trying to be a friend instead of what he'd expected and hoped they would be. Lovers, partners, parents. It killed him to think of that.

He'd considered skipping the wedding, almost called his mom in Spring Valley a dozen times, but at the last minute he'd held himself back. He needed to go home anyway. For one thing, his mom had told him that they were expecting to get an offer in the days after the wedding, and Tom was planning to leave for Boston then, too. He had to be there.

And he'd told Amy the truth when he said he wanted to be part of the baby's life, which meant he needed to be able to spend time with her, as much as it hurt.

He could only hope that it would hurt less over time.

Jack brought himself back to the present, where he was sitting on Benny in an empty paddock. Sam was nowhere to be seen, and Jack was glad of that. He would call and apologize, assure Sam that he'd be in the right headspace when he got back from the wedding. If he spoke to Sam in person right now, there was a chance he'd say something he would regret. Sam was angry enough that Jack knew it would be nearly impossible to have a rational conversation with him.

Jack slid off Benny and walked him into the barn. Once the horse was settled in his stall, Jack drove to his new apartment to pack. Even though he'd been in the apartment for several days, he hadn't done a single thing to settle in. It still felt too new, too temporary, whatever he told himself about how he was planning to be here for the long run.

Soon it was time to go, and he only hesitated once more before locking the door.

"Where does this go?" Amy asked, lifting a large pot of flowers and tilting it toward Brock.

"How many times have I told you that I'd get the heavy stuff?" Brock demanded as he grabbed the pot away from her.

Amy rolled her eyes. "It weighs about five pounds, Brock. I'm pregnant, not dying."

Cassie smiled at her from where she stood, decorating an arch for the wedding that was scheduled for the next day. Ever since Amy had told her family about the pregnancy, everyone had been treating her as if she was made of glass, despite Cassie's assurances that Amy was fine.

Amy walked up to her soon-to-be sister. "What can I help you with?"

Cassie shrugged. "Are you sure you have the time?

I know you've been busy planning your own thing like a madwoman."

Amy had been spending every spare moment on her computer or her phone for the past several days. If the wedding was her last chance to win over Jack, she wasn't going to take it lightly. At the same time, she had to make plans for herself and her baby. There was insurance to get, a doctor to find, and so many other details they made Amy's head swim.

But at least she felt as if she was being productive instead of living life by the seat of her pants, basing her decisions on her selfish feelings at any given moment.

It was time for her to be a grown-up now.

To Cassie, Amy said, "I've done everything I can do. Now I just need to wait until after the wedding and hope it's enough."

"And if it isn't?" Cassie asked, so quietly Amy almost didn't hear her.

Amy had considered that, too. "If it isn't, I have a life I want to live, and I'll do the best I can with it."

Even if she couldn't win Jack back, Amy knew she had to work hard to give her baby a good life, and that meant she couldn't sit around feeling sorry for herself. She would make it work.

It would be hard to get by without Jack in her life, but she had the confidence in herself now to know she would survive.

But she couldn't think like that. Not yet, anyway. She had to hope.

Amy settled into a spot beside Cassie, helping decorate the arch. "I've got to hand it to you, Cassie, this is going to be a beautiful wedding."

Cassie laughed. "The 'beach in Bali' girl is coming around to my country wedding, huh?"

Amy looked at the wide blue sky then across the ranch, decorated with white chairs and pots of flowers. "I'm more Texas than I used to admit," Amy confessed.

It was the morning of the wedding, and Jack sat at his family's kitchen table, slowly drinking coffee. He wasn't ready to see Amy again in just a few hours, and the fact that it would be at a wedding, something he'd hoped the two of them would have one day, only made it worse.

It had been nearly a week since they'd seen each other, but the pain of it all was still fresh and raw. He was almost thankful that Sam had been working him so hard right up until the day he left because it gave him less time to think. He didn't want to think. Whenever he did, his mind settled on Amy, and it stayed there until he got so busy or tired he couldn't focus on anything.

But now here he was, watching the sky lighten over the home he'd soon be leaving for good, and he had nothing to do but sip his coffee.

He could picture every moment of the last few minutes he'd spent with Amy. The devastation on her face when he'd rejected her. It made his heart ache.

"Morning," Tom said, walking into the kitchen and getting himself some coffee. "You ready for the wedding today?"

Even though Jack had only seen his brother for a few seconds since his encounter with Amy, the way Tom spoke made Jack sure he knew something about what had happened between them. Jack just shrugged. It wasn't something he was ready to talk about.

Besides, there were other topics that needed to be discussed. "Are *you* ready for your big move?" he asked.

Tom was finally leaving for Boston in three days. It made Jack nervous to think his mother would be left on this ranch by herself, but she'd already assured him that she was organizing plenty of help and she didn't need him to worry about her.

Tom looked at his coffee cup and smiled to himself. "I'm ready," he said, not elaborating.

He didn't need to. It was obvious from his expression that he was chomping at the bit to meet this woman from the internet and settle into his new life in Boston. Jack could tell that Tom was over-the-moon in love.

He was happy for his brother, but it also made him wonder if he'd ever feel that way about anybody again.

As if Tom could tell where Jack's mind had gone, he asked, "So, you and Amy are really done for good, huh?"

Jack nodded, as much as it hurt to do so. "If she left again, I don't think I'd be able to take it. It's just safer to stop things now," he explained.

Tom turned toward the stove, away from his brother, and started making breakfast. "So you're happy living in Wyoming, then?" Tom asked over the sound of cracking eggs.

Jack wasn't sure what to say. He didn't want to lie to his brother, but there was no point complaining about the choice he'd made, and if he could make a big purse before his mother accepted an offer on the ranch, then maybe he could still make his rodeo school dream come true. "I'm starting to settle in," he said carefully.

Tom nodded, and Jack thought for a moment that the conversation was done. "And Sam? Is he a good partner?"

Again, Jack chose his words cautiously. "He is an incredibly skilled rider and roper. And he's very dedicated."

Tom turned from the stove and looked at his younger brother. "So long as you're happy with your decisions, that's all that matters," he said before turning back and pouring eggs into a sizzling pan. "You want some breakfast?" he asked over his shoulder.

"No thanks," Jack said.

He felt antsy, like he needed to go do some thinking. He stood and walked over to the back door, where he had a view of the barn and paddocks. The chances that he could keep this place, especially with an offer coming in over the next couple of days, according to his mom, were slim to none. If he couldn't save the ranch, what would he do with any big purses he won while riding with Sam?

Jack knew it was time to be realistic about his future, and the more he looked at it, the less he liked what he saw. But he needed Sam, didn't he? Otherwise he'd just be a failed roper with a few dollars to his name and no prospects.

Jack walked to the barn and went up to Maverick, who seemed to be looking over Jack's shoulder for someone. "She's not here, boy," Jack told the horse.

Maverick seemed crestfallen. Jack knew how the animal felt. After a minute of brushing the sleek black horse, Jack started talking. "There's not much chance working with Sam will get me the ranch, Maverick, and I can't ask my family to hold off living their lives while I try to make enough money to have it happen, but without that, what do I have?"

Jack had no idea, and Maverick didn't seem forthcoming with any alternatives, either. Jack kept brushing the horse, wondering what kind of a life would make him happy.

Nothing came to him. Maverick snorted and tossed his head, and Jack patted the animal once more before turning back toward the house.

AMY LOOKED OVER the crowd from her vantage point of Cassie's bedroom window, a bouquet in her hand. There were nearly three hundred people taking their seats: an interesting mix of Spring Valley residents, Brock's rodeo buddies and Cassie's family from Minnesota standing out among the sea of cowboy hats. Even among all those people, it only took her a second to see Jack sitting with the rest of his family.

She wanted so badly to rush over to him, but managed to hold herself back. This was Brock and Cassie's wedding, and she had a job to do. At the reception, they would be able to talk. That was when she would have her chance.

And if it went wrong or he just decided not to be with her, well, she'd handle it. Amy put a hand to her stomach and said a little prayer, then turned to where Cassie stood with her two other bridesmaids, her sister from Minnesota and Emma, who ran the local bakery. Cassie was brushing her hands along the skirt of her wedding dress, looking a little nervous.

"Are you ready, sister?" Amy asked her, putting a hand on her shoulder.

Cassie nodded and Amy gave her a brief hug. "Let's go get you married, then," she said, and the four women trooped out of the room. Soon they were all walking down the aisle toward where Brock, Jose, Diego, Zach and Carter stood, the younger twins looking especially proud in their suits.

Amy tried to keep her mind focused on the ceremony, but she couldn't stop herself from glancing at Jack every few minutes. Every time she did, her heart thumped hard and painful against her chest. Twice, their eyes met, and it only made things worse.

Did he miss her, or was he truly satisfied with just being friends? She couldn't tell by his small smile or the look in his blue eyes.

When it came time for the vows, though, all off Amy's attention was on the bride and groom. Brock held Cassie's hands in his and said, "Cassie, you are everything I could imagine in a wife, and you make me a better man. I feel so honored that you would let me into your life and become a part of your family. I love you more every day, and I want to be with you always."

Tears streamed down Amy's face. She was so happy her brother had found someone to love who wanted to spend her life with him.

Amy could only hope to be so lucky. She risked one more glance at Jack, but his eyes were on the couple.

Soon the wedding was over, and the guests moved toward the barn, where scattered tables circled an open area that was clearly meant for a dance floor. Even though it was late October, the air was almost warm and the flowers scattered everywhere gave it a summery atmosphere.

Amy started walking toward Jack. This was it. She would be able to speak to him before the reception truly got started, and then she would know, for better or worse. On her way, though, she was waylaid by Jose and Diego, who had arrived after she'd gone to stay over with Cassie and the bridesmaids the night before the wedding.

Jose picked her up and squeezed her in a tight hug. "Congratulations!" he shouted so loudly that several guests turned to stare.

Amy would've felt embarrassed by Jose's outburst, but he'd done something like that to her so many times that it had ceased to be surprising. Right now, she was just a little annoyed. She was a woman on a mission.

"Set me down, Jose," she said, hitting him on the shoulder to show she meant business.

Jose set her down and Diego said, "We heard about what's going on. Good luck, Ames."

The endearing nickname made her heart twist. If Jack rejected her once more, she wasn't sure she could stand to hear anyone call her that again. "Thanks, Diego. I'll come talk to you two and Kate when I'm done," she told them.

"Kate couldn't come," Jose said, "but I expect a long sincere conversation with my sister about why she doesn't let me in on all her interesting gossip."

Amy nodded. If things didn't go the way she wanted, it might be hard to have normal conversations, but she had vowed to be less selfish, and this would be the perfect test.

Then she left her brothers and continued on her way. As she closed in on Jack, it became hard to breathe. Part of her wanted to run away, but she held fast. She was done running from her problems.

JACK COULD HARDLY keep himself still as the wedding guests moved around him, finding their seats and chatting with friends. He knew Amy was walking toward him, her eyes focused and unwavering. She looked different, somehow, than the last time he'd seen her. There was a sense of calm around her he couldn't explain.

"JACK," SHE SAID IN a sighing breath that made his heart ache. "Can I speak to you for a minute? Privately?"

Jack agreed and followed her toward Cassie's house, though he found it difficult to make his feet move. There was so much unsaid between them, and he wasn't sure if he was ready for this even though he'd known it was coming.

Before they could get too far, however, Amy's ma walked up with a woman about her age and Cassie's young twins in tow. Based on the fact that she was a nearly identical older version of Cassie, Jack guessed this must be Brock's new mother-in-law. She had on a sour expression that made Jack wonder how hard she'd fought to stop this wedding.

"Amy, Jack!" Amy's mother said with a big smile. "I'm showing Cassie's mom around the place, giving her a chance to see all that Spring Valley has to offer to these young'uns and their parents."

Jack turned to Amy. He saw her hesitate and knew she wanted to keep going, but then she gave the women a big smile. "Spring Valley is home, ma'am. I've traveled all over the world, but there's no place else like it."

Her gaze turned to Jack as she finished, and he knew her words were for him as much as for Cassie's mother. He watched her, speechless, as she quickly extolled the virtues of Texas, gave the young boys hugs and then continued on their path to the house.

Who was this woman? It was Amy, but with a new demeanor he couldn't understand. He didn't know if it had to do with the pregnancy or his rejection of her, but he watched her closely as they walked through the ranch home's back door that led them into the kitchen.

"I want to buy the ranch," Amy said the moment they were through the back door of the empty house.

"What?" Jack asked, sure he hadn't heard her correctly.

Of all the things he'd guessed she might say once they were alone, this was a complete surprise.

"I want to buy your family's ranch. I have some cash saved up, plus a loan from my parents. It's enough to get a mortgage on the place. Tom would get his fair share, and your mom would like to continue living on the ranch and put her portion into helping me turn the place into a rodeo school. With help from Jose and Diego I can get the stock, and Brock and my uncle Joe will gladly help get rodeo hopefuls out here."

Jack stared at her, uncomprehending. What was she saying?

"I can make your dream a reality, Jack, and I want to do it. I want to live here, on a ranch with horses and family close by. Brock and I can manage the place as long as you're on the circuit. I'll still be able to do some writing for magazines I know would love to hear about Texas life. And I'll be here with the baby when you're ready to take over. I'm not running again, Jack. If I get on a plane, I want you to be there by my side," she finished, handing him a stack of papers.

Amy took a deep breath, as if she'd just given a speech she'd been preparing for a long time. Which, it seemed, was pretty accurate.

Jack quickly rifled through the pile of documents. It included an offer for the ranch, a purchase order of rodeo stock and a passport application with his name already filled in.

He didn't know what to say. Jack looked up at Amy, who was shifting nervously. "Are you really ready for all this?" he asked, gesturing to the papers.

Amy nodded with conviction. "I think all these years I've been traveling, I've been looking for something. A home, a place to be, something. When I was in Thailand, though, I wasn't looking for that because I'd already found it here, with you, on your ranch. I was miserable so far from the people, the person, I love. I know what I want now, and this is it," she said, gesturing toward the documents.

Jack didn't need to hear any more. He tossed the papers onto the table and pulled Amy into a long, tender kiss that left them both breathless. After, he pressed his forehead against hers, taking in her sweet flowery smell and staring into the endless depths of her eyes. "I love you, Amy McNeal," he said softly.

Amy sighed and closed her eyes. "No 'but' this time?" she asked, as if she couldn't be sure this was real.

He shook his head while still leaning it against hers so hers shook as well. "No 'but,' Ames," he said softly. "Never again. I have a ring for you back at the ranch. A ring that's been waiting for you for ten years. Will you marry me?"

Amy let out a long sigh that was all the answer he needed. They shared another deep kiss. "I want to be the woman you deserve," she told him.

Jack felt his heart go tight with love for her. "You're everything and more," he reassured her, giving her a last squeeze before realizing it was probably time to go back out among the other guests.

As they walked back to the wedding together, Amy leaned against Jack. "When do you need to go back to Wyoming?" she asked.

Jack smiled. "I don't, actually, except for a quick trip to get Benny and my things," he said.

When she stopped walking and gave him a look of confusion, he explained, "I called and quit this morning. Wyoming isn't where I want to be. I want to be here in Spring Valley. I always have. Money might be a little tight for a while, but—"

"But we'll make it work," she finished for him.

He planted one more kiss on her lips, unable to stop himself. "Let's dance," he said with a smile as they threaded through the wedding guests toward the dance floor.

They had so much to celebrate.

Epilogue

Amy watched the paper lantern lift into the sky, the small fire beneath it propelling the entire thing up to join the others, thousands of them looking like so many stars in the darkness. She leaned close to Jack, staying silent until she could no longer see which lantern was theirs. "So, what do you think?" she asked him as she looked across the throng of people celebrating the festival.

Jack gave her a little squeeze. "Way better than Bastille Day in Paris."

Amy nodded in agreement, her eyes still on the sky as her thoughts drifted to their daughter and son, so far away.

"You're thinking about Spring Valley, aren't you?" Jack asked her, his cornflower blue eyes studying her face.

She smiled. He always knew when she was missing home. "Darcy would love this," she told him, picturing their four-year-old daughter shrieking with delight as the lantern flew away, her blue eyes sparkling just like her father's were.

"She would," Jack said, "and we'll definitely need to bring her and Archer when they're a little older. For now, I'm sure they're perfectly content getting spoiled rotten by all three grandparents. Remember how happy Archer was when we did that video call this morning?"

Amy knew he was right, but she was still itching to see them. Archer had only been adopted the year before, and it still felt odd to leave him for a few days, no matter how good of hands he was in. "You don't think they're jealous that Jessie got to come?" she asked, putting a hand on the small swell of her belly.

"By the time we've given them all their gifts, I'm not sure they'll even remember we were gone for any reason other than to buy them stuff. It's a good thing the rodeo school is doing so well or we might need a second mortgage on the ranch to pay for this trip."

Amy knocked him playfully with her shoulder. "Those are business expenses. I'm going to write a great article series on how to haggle."

They stood silently as another hundred lanterns joined the rest, then Jack asked, "Should we get back to the hotel?"

Amy nodded. "My feet are exhausted. Just one last thing," she said, diving into the crowd.

She was back a minute later with at least a dozen more paper lanterns piled in a big stack. "Now we can have our own little festival in Spring Valley," she explained.

Jack gave her a wide grin. "The kids will love them," he said.

Amy agreed. "Everyone will have a great time lighting them off. That, or someone will burn the house down. Either way, it'll be a good story. And we have insurance that covers paper lanterns lit on fire, right?"

Jack laughed and shook his head at his wife's silly sense of humor. "I love you, Amy McNeal-Stuart," he said, wrapping his arms around her.

They kissed, and the noise and crowds of the festival faded away as they held each other.

* * * * *

If you loved this book, look for the previous book in Ali Olson's SPRING VALLEY, TEXAS *series:*

THE BULL RIDER'S TWIN TROUBLE

And more, available now at Harlequin.com!

We hope you enjoyed this story from
Harlequin® Western Romance.

Harlequin® Western Romance is coming to an end, but community, cowboys and true love are here to stay. Starting July 2018, discover more heartfelt tales of family and friendship from **Harlequin® Special Edition**.

Romance is for life, and these stories show that every chapter in a relationship has its challenges and delights and that love can be renewed with each turn of the page!

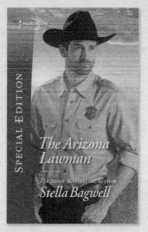

Look for six *new* romances every month from **Harlequin® Special Edition!**
Available wherever books are sold.

HWRST0318

Eyes widening, she gasped. "Ryder."

"Hello, Becca."

"Hi." Her gaze darted briefly to the small boy next to her. "This is a surprise."

"That's an understatement." Ryder did a quick mental calculation. The boy would've been two years old when Becca's grandmother died. As far as he knew, Shirley hadn't mentioned anything about Becca having a kid. And when it came to what little news they got about Amy and Becca in LA, his mom never skipped a word.

"Right." She cleared her throat. "I planned on calling you and your mom later."

He raised his eyebrows.

"You know, after we settled in. We just got to town an hour ago."

Okay, maybe she was telling the truth. But why look so nervous? "I hope by *we* you mean Amy," he said, holding Becca's gaze. "Is she here?"

She shook her head. Sadness flickered in her hazel eyes before she blinked and looked away. "I think she had other plans for the—" She pressed her lips together and swallowed.

"What? For Thanksgiving? Let's see, that makes seven of them that she's missed now?"

"I'm not her keeper," Becca said, her voice barely a whisper. "Your sister does what she wants."

"Aunt Amy gave me a neato truck." The kid grinned up at him. "You wanna see it?"

Ryder felt a surge of relief. He didn't know what had given him the sick feeling that something bad had happened to Amy. If that were true, she wouldn't be buying the kid toys. "Hey, sport."

"Sport?" The boy wrinkled his nose. "My name is Noah."

"Sorry, Noah. I'm Ryder." He stuck his hand out. The kid slapped his palm against Ryder's and started giggling.

In spite of himself, Ryder smiled. Whatever was up with Amy wasn't Becca's son's fault. Ryder was seven years older than his sister and hadn't paid much attention to her friends, but he remembered Becca.

When he looked back up at her, he saw the tears in her eyes before she blinked them away.

The relief he'd felt moments ago disappeared. Something was wrong, and Becca knew the truth.

*Don't miss TO TRUST A RANCHER by Debbi Rawlins, available May 2018 wherever Harlequin®
Western Romance books and ebooks are sold.*

www.Harlequin.com